The Trustee

Jim Flynn

ISBN: 9798794352931

By the same author:

Overdraft

Where There's No Will

Fraudulent Transfers

A Compendium of Curious Colorado Place Names

Jim Flynn's Best of Money & the Law

Chapter 1

"Jack," my receptionist said over the office intercom, "Scott Freeman called and was hoping you could meet him for an adult beverage at the Antelope Hotel lobby bar at around 5:00. Are you OK with that? If so, I'll call him back and confirm."

"Yes, Linda. Tell him that's fine. I'll meet him there. Did he say what's on the agenda?"

"No. He just said, as usual, that it was important and that he needed your help."

It was now 4:30 and, although I should have been working on the closing argument for a case coming up for trial in a week, I was instead trying out a new recipe for an Adams 12, one of my favorite trout flies. My fondness for this fly began years ago when I met a man fishing on the East River just upstream from its confluence with the Taylor River, where the East and the Taylor come together at the town of Almont to form the Gunnison River. He was catching fish on nearly every cast, and I was catching nothing. So, I finally swallowed my pride and asked him what fly he was using.

"Adams 12," he said. "Never use anything else. Here. I have a bunch. Try it out." He gave me one of his, which had been beautifully tied. I put the fly on my line and, sure enough, I started catching fish. The Adams 12, which imitates maybe mayflies and maybe caddis flies and who knows what else, is certainly not the only fly I use, but I'll never go fishing again without a supply of them in my fly box. The new recipe I was trying used synthetic material as opposed to traditional fur and feathers. In theory, at least, this would produce a fly that would float better and not get water-logged and sink. But, the synthetic material was harder to work with, and convinced me I needed stronger glasses.

At 4:55, I tucked my fly tying gear away in a desk drawer and replaced it, on my desk top, with a couple of law books, the keyboard for my computer, a fresh legal pad, two newly sharpened no. 2 pencils, and the file for the case I should have been working on, thereby restoring the appearance of my desk to that of a busy lawyer doing what he was supposed to be doing. I was confident that my partners here at McConnell Jones and Knight, Bruce Jones and Jennifer Knight, would not be shocked to find fly tying material on my desk but, still, I thought I should do my part to make our office look professional.

The Antelope Hotel was only a block away and Scott Freeman was already there when I arrived. Scott and I, both just turned 60, have been friends and respected professional colleagues for thirty-plus years. We first met, as young lawyers, when we were on opposite sides of a hotly disputed will contest. That case was finally resolved in an exhausting two-week jury trial, which my side won. In that trial, Scott proved himself a most worthy and ethical opponent, and we have been good friends, and sending each other business, ever since.

Scott, having learned that go-to-court lawyers live a life of intense stress and are regularly called on to give clients psychiatric counseling in addition to legal advice, had, after the trial we shared, chosen to limit his practice to estate planning and he had become a nationally known expert in the field. He has both a law degree from Yale and a master's degree in taxation from the University of

Chicago, and he helps people all over the country -- in fact, all over the world -- put in place strategies to pass their wealth on to future generations and charitable enterprises with minimal diminution from taxes.

Scott is a senior partner at a big multi-state/multi-national law firm – Jensen & Kirkpatrick. He heads up what he calls the firm's death and taxes department. That department generates millions of dollars in income every year and, in appreciation, the firm lets Scott practice out of whichever of its many offices he chooses. He chose Colorado Springs because of a life-long battle with asthma and the fact that Colorado Springs' dry climate helps this condition. Scott's production of revenue is recognized within his firm and appreciated when the time comes to divide up profits, and Scott enjoys a seven-figure income. Nonetheless, he lives a simple life and generously supports charities whose causes he believes in. Scott also runs his firm's pro bono program and the firm, world wide, encourages and rewards pro bono work. Scott himself spends at least one day a month at the Colorado Springs Senior Center helping people, without charge, prepare simple wills and "advance directives" – financial powers of attorney, living wills, and do not resuscitate instructions for people who don't want to be brought back to life if their heart stops.

Scott doesn't impress physically. He's maybe five foot nine, overweight to a noticeable degree, balding and with thick-lensed bifocals. But when he speaks, you know you are in the presence of a highly intelligent, thoughtful, caring man.

"Hi McConnell. Thanks for coming on short notice. I was afraid you'd be off fishing somewhere."

"Hi Scott. Good to see you. No, the rivers are still swollen with snowmelt, so it's not quite prime fishing season yet and besides I've been having to spend far too much time in the office doing actual legal work. As you know, my clients, more than yours, are busy fighting over money they wish they had, or want to keep, and I am at the mercy of court clerks who tell me when I have to be somewhere and do something. But, it's good to see you again. As we keep telling each other, we should get together more often, just for fun, instead of responding to external events. Which, I assume, is what has generated this meeting and not, say, a desire to discuss the Rockies' bullpen."

"Correct, but let's order a drink and then I'll tell you what legal quicksand I've found myself in this time."

At this point, the bartender, an aging but still attractive lady named Allie, came to our booth, informed us of the opportunities provided by happy hour, and solicited our order.

"I'll have a glass of your house Merlot," I said.

"Same for me," Scott said.

"Scott, what happened to your exacting ingredients martini, which you have been ordering here for decades?"

"Well Jack, my doctor -- our doctor, Rollie Dumbarton -- told me if I wanted to avoid serious risk of a cardiovascular accident like, say, a stroke or a myocardial infarction, I either had to cut down on drinking or start exercising regularly. He wanted me to do both. We then had a negotiation. I agreed to accept one or the other of his recommendations – not both -- but only if he agreed to have the colonoscopy he's been avoiding since you and I first met him, during the Carter administration. In any event, faced with this difficult choice, I elected to give up martinis. This has not been easy, mind you. We'll see how it goes."

"OK, so what's up that you need a lawyer?"

"Oh Jack, it's a long and complicated story as usual, but it involves a woman named Maria Thurston, both a friend and a client. Maria, forty years ago, hitched up with a wealthy man named Andrew Thurston. This was a first marriage for Maria and a second marriage for Andy. Andy, who had a Ph.D. in pharmacology from the University of Texas, started, and eventually took public, a retail drug store company called PharmOne Drugs. Its stock is listed on the New York Stock Exchange under the symbol PODR. You've probably seen its stores here in Colorado Springs – there are four of them -- and seen it advertised nationally online and on television. Andy had two sons by his first marriage, Duane and William, so they became Maria's stepsons. Maria and Andy together sired a third son, Phillip. Duane, who also has a degree in pharmacology from the University of Texas, has grown up to be a scoundrel. William – Billie, he's called – is intellectually challenged, never made it out of high school and seems to do whatever Duane tells him to do. Duane knows the pharmacology world well, having worked for his father for several years as a purchaser of inventory for the PharmOne stores. So, Andy dies three years ago of a heart attack resulting from a lifetime of executive stress. He leaves each of his three sons PODR stock worth, at the time of his death, roughly three million dollars. The rest of his estate, which included another $290 million in PODR stock and four homes – one in Vail, one in San Clemente, one in San Antonio and one here in Colorado Springs collectively worth maybe ten million dollars -- goes into a trust, the Thurston Family

Trust. The trust document says the trust is to support Maria
for the rest of her life and then whatever is left when she dies
is to go 10% to each of Andy's three kids -- roughly $30
million per kid -- and the rest -- roughly $210 million -- is to
go into a charitable foundation, whose purpose will be to
support cutting edge pharmaceutical research. That would
all be OK except that the trust agreement names Maria as the
successor trustee -- to take over trustee duties at Andy's
death -- and it gives her total discretion to change how the
trust assets are distributed, both during her lifetime and at
her death. So, she basically was given the power to change
the distribution of Andy's wealth as she saw fit. And, she
has seen fit to give Duane and Billie a major haircut and
shift most of what was originally going to be their share of
the trust's assets at her death into the charitable foundation.
To oversimplify a bit, Maria's decision along those lines is
costing Duane and Billie $27 million each, leaving each of
them with maybe $3 million instead of $30 million. Phillip's
share, however, was not affected by Maria's actions, so he's
still in line to receive roughly $30 million out of the trust
when Maria dies, although a sizeable chunk of that will be
set aside for Phillip's two kids."

   "So, Scott, what does this have to do with you – and,
apparently, me?"

   "Well, McConnell, first of all, I was acting as
Maria's lawyer when she, as successor trustee after Andy's
death, decided to amend the trust agreement for the Thurston
Family Trust and thereby greatly reduce Duane's and
Billie's distributions from the trust. I also agreed to serve as
the trustee of the Thurston Family Trust after Maria dies, and
that's not far off. Until she dies, she's the trustee and
Duane's legal bullets can all be shot at her. But, when she's

gone, I move up to the front line. I'm also responsible for creating the Thurston Family Foundation, and serving as its first CEO, when Maria dies. In any event, at Maria's direction, I drafted the amendment to the trust agreement that gave Duane and Billie their haircut."

"Oh boy, here we go again. You promised me after the Cranston estate litigation we worked through together that you would never again agree to serve as anyone's trustee. So what happened here to cause you to forget the misery you went through as trustee of the Cranston trust?"

"Yeah, I know I said that, but Maria and Andy had been clients – and friends – for decades and, well, Maria begged me to agree to be the next in line trustee of the Thurston Family Trust, and to organize the Thurston Family Foundation and be its CEO, when she dies. Have you ever tried to say no to someone dying of pancreatic cancer who is asking you – pleading with you -- for help in regard to a really important matter?"

"OK, fine. I get it. But, again, what does this have to do with me?"

"As soon as Maria dies, there is going to be legal warfare including, I believe, a lawsuit filed against me personally. And Jack, I need you to be my lawyer – the lawyer who defends the actions Maria has taken and I have taken -- and will be taking -- as having been just and proper. I need you to be the lawyer who defends my honor and reputation and who protects me from Duane Thurston's claim that I am the unethical, evil, greedy jerk he will portray me to be in the litigation I expect to happen after Maria's death. And I need you to help me carry out my fiduciary duty, and moral duty, to see Maria's wishes carried out."

"And what about Phillip? How does he fit into this drama?"

"Unfortunately, Phillip is congenitally incapable of managing money. He is divorced and his two kids are now in their early teens. He's never held a meaningful job his whole life and has basically lived off the generosity of Andy and, to a lesser extent, Maria. In any event, his kids are Maria's only grandchildren, and she loves them dearly. And she is convinced that Phillip, if left to his own unsupervised devices, will manage to piss away his entire inheritance, leaving his kids penniless and living under a bridge. It took Phillip only eighteen months to blow through the entire $3 million inheritance he received when Andy died. For these reasons, the changes Maria has made to the trust agreement for the Thurston Family Trust have put Phillip on a short leash. He has to live on a budget approved by the trustee and he can't buy or sell anything of consequence without the trustee's consent, meaning, after Maria dies, my consent. Also, the trust agreement, as amended, requires the trustee to give priority to the needs of Phillip's kids, to include their education and a sound financial footing after they're done with college. So I'll have some discretionary decision making on that front as well."

"You really haven't learned anything from the Cranston litigation, have you."

"I've learned, or relearned, that I want you on my team when legal fireworks begin that are going to disrupt what I have wanted to be a nice tranquil intellectually stimulating estate planning practice involving appreciative clients with normal children and challenging tax issues."

"OK, assuming I let you talk me into this engagement, what happens next?"

"I want you to meet Maria. She's now at a hospice facility here in town run by the Sisters of Mercy. I'll check with your secretary and set up a meeting."

Just at this time in our conversation, Allie cycled back to our booth to see how we were doing. "I'll have another glass of the house Merlot," I said. Scott, after a pause, ordered a martini, with his exacting ingredients. I resisted the temptation to comment on this breach of his contract with his – our -- doctor. I did, however, give him my best scowl. We then turned our attention to the Rockies bullpen where, as usual, there was no reason for optimism as the new season begins to unfold.

Chapter 2

Scott set up our meeting with Maria for the following Thursday, at 4:00 p.m., so we wouldn't be rushed by end of the day interruptions. I dutifully arrived at the hospice facility on time and met Scott in the lobby. This was not a pleasant experience for me, knowing that everyone staying in this place was there because they were dying. I don't do well with death. Ten years ago, I lost my only sibling, an older sister who was a Stanford educated doctor, in a helicopter crash when she and the crew of the helicopter were trying to rescue the crew of a Japanese fishing boat that ran aground and sank off Point Lobos, south of Carmel, during a huge winter storm. All members of the helicopter crew, and all those on the fishing boat, were lost, with no bodies ever recovered. They were doubtless ground to bits by the pounding surf and eaten by fish.

Then, shortly after that, both my parents had died, one from myeloma and the other from a massive stroke, and a broken heart. And most recently, I had to deal with the death of Fletcher, my Labrador retriever who had been my constant companion for twelve years. My vet made a house call for that event, and together we put Fletcher down in the gentle manner reserved only for pets. I'll never forget the final wag of his tail, telling me, I believe, he understood what we were doing and thanking me for rescuing him from the pain he had been suffering. He was cremated with two of his favorite sticks and I spread his ashes along the banks of a small stream that comes down off the northeast slope of

Mount Sherman where we had many good days together, with me catching beautifully colored high mountain brook trout and Fletcher chasing after chipmunks, and an occasional marmot, which he never caught.

Maria was sitting up in bed, leaning on an assembly of pillows, when we entered her room. She was 75 years old, Scott would later tell me, but she looked somewhat younger, thanks, no doubt, to help from cosmetic surgery. She had on a cheery looking nightgown with various animal images, notably giraffes, and she was wearing makeup, applied, I assumed, in anticipation of our visit. Her hair had been colored, to a muted brown, and cut short, although the gray was showing through. Notwithstanding the makeup, Maria looked pale. She also looked shriveled, weighing I would guess no more than 90 pounds. I estimated her height at maybe five foot four, although it was hard to tell since she was in bed and under the covers.

She greeted us with a weak smile and a feeble handshake, and Scott took charge of the introduction. "Maria, this is Jack McConnell, an old friend and a great lawyer who, although he should know better, engages in that part of the practice of law that involves dispute resolution – a trial lawyer. Not the kind that chases ambulances in pursuit of contingent fees but rather a lawyer who helps clients try to resolve complex legal issues through negotiation and mediation, and uses the courts when all else fails. Jack, not too long ago, represented me in another difficult trust dispute and, since we think that's where we're heading with your situation, I have wanted him to be a part of the team."

"Hello Maria. I'm glad to meet you. Scott has told me quite a bit about you and how you want Andy's trust to operate, and the problems that might arise. I'm honored to be of service."

"So Maria," Scott said, "tell Jack what your concerns have come to be about Duane and Billie, and Phillip."

At this point, tears came to Maria's eyes and her words came slowly, and with difficulty. "I tried to be a good mother to my stepsons but as soon as I arrived on the scene, Duane was hateful of me, and soon became hateful of Andy. Maybe this was the result of losing his real mother, who died in a car accident when he was seven. But I also think he was born with a chip on his shoulder for everyone and everything. And he's carried that into his adult life. He's never really used his college degree to hold down a responsible job. His latest employment has been as the CFO of a taxi company operating in Austin and Colorado Springs. He has been physically abusive to the women he's occasionally hung out with, none of whom ever lasted long enough to become a possible life companion and, after Andy's death, he has generated a small police record of domestic violence to show for it. He has never missed an opportunity to disparage his father and me to other people, except when he needed money, and then he could be charming for as long as it took to meet his immediate objectives. I have no real proof of this but I think Duane is somehow involved in drug trafficking. Just things I've noticed since Andy's death, and things Billie has said. The way Andy's estate planning was set up, I am now the custodian of his wealth and I know, if Andy were still alive, he would not want to see a material part of his wealth pass to a child who was involved in criminal drug activities, was disrespectful of him and of me, and would spend his inheritance on self-indulgence. Andy cared deeply about the foundation he wanted created and, once there's no longer any need to take care of me, that's where he would want the bulk of his wealth to go. And that's what I have wanted to see happen, and why I amended the trust agreement of the Thurston Family Trust to that end. And now, I need you two to be sure it does happen."

"And what about Billie?" I asked.

"Billie suffers from a developmental disability. He has a below average IQ and has always failed at educational opportunities, and we have tried them all. The only person he has let into his life is Duane, and not me or Andy or Phillip. Duane has managed to milk this relationship for his own benefit, to include an occasional undocumented loan from Billie, never to be repaid. Billie actually has some talent as an artist but Duane has seen to it that this talent has never been allowed to develop. My hopes for Billie involve getting him out from under the control of Duane and giving him a chance at a quiet life where he can be safe, and paint. The Thurston Family Trust, as I have amended it, will, after my death, allow him this opportunity. But without this amendment, any wealth coming to Billie would, I believe, have ended up being controlled by Duane, and I didn't want that to happen and I'm convinced Andy also would not have wanted that to happen."

"And tell Jack about Phillip," Scott said.

By now it was clear Maria was tiring and her words came ever more slowly.

"Well, Phillip is my own flesh and blood, which complicates the landscape. He is now forty years old and is trying to raise two teenage children – a boy and a girl – born from a marriage that didn't work out. They're good kids and have a chance to make it to college and then, at least by Thurston family standards, have a normal life. Phillip never made it to college and has muddled along with various jobs, mostly in real estate property management. The Thurston Family Trust has provided him with enough income to allow him to own a nice home and drive a nice car. But he is always on my doorstep looking for more money and whatever I let him have is quickly gone, thanks to frivolous purchases. My plans for him involve adequate support, and money to send his kids to college and to get a start in life after that. But, no big unrestricted distributions that he can fritter away. I've amended the Thurston Family Trust in pursuant of those objectives, with Scott in charge as trustee to, after I'm gone, carry out the plan."

By now, Maria was seriously fading, so Scott asked if there was anything we could do to help her be more comfortable. "Thanks Scott. No, they take good care of me here. I talk a lot with the staff about death. They're very honest and tell me that what's in store for me will be a quiet shut down of important organs – lungs, heart, brain, kidneys – which will push me into a pre-death coma, which could last a few hours or a few days. But, as between the coma and the drugs they'll be giving me, there won't be any pain. At some point, my heart will stop, my body will no longer be receiving oxygen or nutrients, and that will be that. I'll mostly sleep through the final act, which could be tomorrow or a few weeks from now. My medical instructions, as Scott knows since he wrote them for me, are -- no heroics. Just let me go. Not even fluid IV's. I'm not afraid of death and I'm not counting on any afterlife. If there is a god, he or she -- or it -- has failed to deal with the world's problems in any useful way and is impotent and irrelevant. What I mostly worry about now are all the decisions that will need to be made after I'm gone and, Scott, that's where you come in. After our many years of friendship, you know me better than anyone else and I know you will know what decisions I would make if I still had my hand on the wheel or the tiller or whatever it is. That gives me great comfort as I push on to the end."

At this point, Maria closed her eyes and put out her hand, which Scott took gently and held. She then went to sleep. We waited silently for a few minutes and left the room.

I made it home, which wasn't far from the hospice, a little before 6:00. The sun had already disappeared behind Pikes Peak but the evening chill had not yet set in and the air was still warm. Cooper, a now 21-year-old neighbor of mine and a friend, in his junior year at the University of Colorado in Boulder, was sitting on my front porch, drinking a beer he had taken from my refrigerator. This continued a tradition that went back several years, since the days Cooper was in high school, hopelessly in love with a girl named Samantha and looking for advice from an adult male about women. I told him my credentials were limited in this regard but he didn't seem to mind. When we were having these conversations, I would allow him an occasional beer with the understanding that he would not breathe in the vicinity of his parents when he went home.

While he was still in high school and living at home, Cooper would take care of Fletcher and my house while I was out of town or working late at the office. Cooper's parents were nice people but he didn't seem to bond with them when the time came to talk about serious things like, say, women. And, once Veronica came into my life, not withstanding my denials, he considered me a source of reliable information.

"Hi Coop. Home for the weekend?" I asked, joining him on the porch.

"Yeah. I don't much like hanging around the campus on weekends. CU turns into the party school it prides itself on being and there's not much room for people like me who would rather be in the library studying."

"Speaking of studying, how's it going?"

"I've been on the Dean's list every semester, so I think that's good. I had a little trouble with calculus but I finally figured it out and scrambled to a B."

"Yes, that is certainly good performance and congratulations. Plus, I doubt you'll ever find the need for calculus in your life. Did you finally settle on a major?"

"History and French, just like you. And I'm thinking about law school."

"Wow Coop. We need to talk more about law school, and being a lawyer, before you get too far down that path. As I'm sure I told you, I went to law school only to try to avoid being drafted and because I didn't know what else to do with myself, and wanting a few more years to think about it. And here I am, forty years later, still thinking about it and wondering if I made the right decision."

"So Jack, not to change the subject or anything, but you promised to teach me fly fishing and how to tie flies and stuff. What's your timing for that?"

"As soon as the rivers settle down a bit, we'll be heading out. I have a fly rod for you I don't use much anymore and an old pair of boots and waders. We're going to start you out on Beaver Creek, a small stream on the west side of Pikes Peak, not too far from Cripple Creek, with a healthy population of hungry but mostly small brown trout. And we'll see if you have fun. If so, I'll set you up with a beginner fly tying kit and we'll get you working on some basic flies, like a hare's ear, which looks like a piece of brown fuzz but still catches fish. Hey, I need to get inside and catch up on emails, but how's it going with Samantha?"

"Oh man, Jack, she dumped me three weeks ago. She went to some fraternity party and ended up with a tight end on the football team lusting after her. Six foot four, 230 pounds. A hunk, as opposed to me, the weenie. This guy is dumber than a skunk – no, the skunks around here at least are smarter than he is – but he's a campus celebrity, headed for the pros they say."

"Sorry to hear that Coop. As you may recall, we discussed this possibility on several occasions and what might be an appropriate response. And, how did you do?"

"Well, as you had instructed, I told Samantha I loved her and wanted her to be happy. Then I went to my dorm room, shut the door, didn't come out for three days, and cried my eyes out. And I eventually remembered your words of wisdom about other fish in the pond, or whatever it was, and decided I needed to get on with my life. So I started looking around at other girls, but so far I haven't had the courage to talk to any of them. There's only a limited amount of rejection I can handle in a short period of time."

"Just be yourself, Coop. It will work out – for the best, Veronica always tells me. Here, give me your beer can. I still don't think your parents recycle. Tell them I said hello."

It continued to be hard coming home to my house without Fletcher there to greet me and remind me it was time for his dinner. I popped a frozen pizza in the microwave and then headed to my home office to check emails. Nothing of importance, and only one big-reward-for-you opportunity to help Nigerian royalty move money into a U.S. bank account. There was, however, an email from Veronica saying she was still planning to come to Colorado Springs for the weekend and an email from an old fishing friend and retired lawyer, RJ Conover, telling me he was still in Arizona but would be heading back to Colorado as soon as he dealt with a couple of "medical issues" – no details provided. I dashed out a brief reply to both, telling Veronica I was eager for her visit and had a special bottle of wine set aside for the event. I told RJ I'd been checking on his house in nearby Manitou Springs (which, thanks toy Pikes Peak and the Garden of the Gods, is the motel capital of the world…) and all was well, although a family of racoons had moved back into the woodshed next to his garage and had taken up gnawing on the furniture on his deck. I then retrieved my pizza from the microwave and turned on the Rockies game. They were in Kansas City and already behind by five runs in the sixth inning. Since there was no longer a need to take Fletcher out to the fire hydrant for a last nature call, I shut off the TV and headed to bed to read a fishing magazine in a largely unsuccessful effort to flush the practice of law, and what lay ahead for Scott, out of my mind.

Chapter 3

On Monday, after a weekend in the office getting
ready for my upcoming trial but spending a nice Saturday
evening with Veronica watching old movies and Sunday
morning sharing the New York Times, Scott called me to tell
me Maria had died Sunday afternoon, four days after our
visit. She slipped into a pre-death coma at around 2 p.m. and
took her last breath at shortly after 11 p.m. The hospice
nurse on duty that day told Scott Phillip and his two children
came to see Maria around 4 p.m. but by then it was too late
for last words. Duane and Billie were no shows.

After a confrontation about his authority to make last
remains decisions on behalf of Maria, Scott had finally
convinced a local mortuary with a decent reputation to
retrieve her body and arrange for cremation -- her choice.
She told Scott on many occasions she had already taken up
enough space on this overcrowded planet and she no longer
wished to do so in the form of a grave site. Her ashes were
to be commingled with Andy's, which were still in a
carboard box in her basement, and spread at a spot just west
of Colorado Springs, in Pike National Forest, with an
unobstructed and magnificent view of the northeast face of
Pikes Peak. This was a spot she and Andy had frequently
visited and where they could let their dog, Josie, a who-
knows-what sheep dog adopted from the Humane Society,
off leash to roam about and enjoy the smells. Josie's ashes –
she died shortly after Andy – were also in the basement and
were to be spread here as well. Scott had correctly
concluded that spreading human, or canine, ashes on

National Forest land without permission from the U.S.
Forest Service is a criminal act. But, he felt the risks of
prosecution were limited, since gathering evidence would be
difficult, and he was willing to take his chances out of
respect for Maria's wishes.

"So what happens next?" I asked Scott.

"I have a long list of things to attend to. I need to
get Maria's house secure – it's actually an asset of the trust
-- and make sure the lawn watering system is working so the
grass doesn't die; track down her mail and email; and check
to see if the internet logon information she gave me for her
financial and creditor accounts is accurate. I need to take
control of those accounts and see what's going on there. I'll
need access to her financial accounts in order to pay bills and
make investment decisions. Until a death certificate is
issued – which takes several days – this will be a problem
since my efforts will likely be viewed by financial services
firms and creditors as acts of identity theft. But Shelley, my
legal assistant, is great at busting through bureaucracies in
pursuit of a goal line. She has a gift for politely threatening
people who don't do what she asks. Fortunately, Maria, at
my urging, gave me what I hope is correct sign on
information for her computer, her email accounts, and her
financial accounts. So, for the moment, at least, I should be
able to make some progress on this front by going online and
pretending to be her. Identity theft for a good cause. And,
as I had instructed, the checking account she used was in the
name of the trust and she would sign checks as trustee. I can
now sign checks as successor trustee and the bank could care
less. As you probably know after the death of your sister and
your parents, death, as a practical matter, is more

complicated than most people realize, but Maria did a good job of setting things up for a relatively smooth transition."

"So what can I do to help the cause at this point? I assume no one has sued you yet that we know of, although she only died yesterday."

"Shelley and I are going over to Maria's house tomorrow and, if you can, I'd like you to tag along and help me make a video recording of our visit. I fully expect Duane to accuse me of stealing her personal property out of the house."

"Hmm, can we do this late afternoon? I have a trial starting on Wednesday, so I'll be scrambling tomorrow to pull everything together for that."

"Jack, I really think you should flush this litigation stuff and shift over to a nice quiet life as an estate planner. Although it will be a challenge – old dog new tricks – I think I can teach you what you would need to know."

"Thanks Scott. We've had this conversation before. I would miss the excitement of living on the edge of uncertainty and the courtroom combat. Plus, your life as an estate planner doesn't seem all that quiet to me. Like, I bet your clients do a lousy job of telling you when they're going to die. I've rarely had to worry about that."

"Whatever. I'll see you at Maria's place at 4:00 tomorrow. The address is 1427 Victoria Drive, on the west side of the Broadmoor Hotel. And after that, you can help me with a trip to the site where Maria's and Andy's and Josie's ashes are to be spread. You know that area, since you and Fletcher hiked there a lot. I've never been close to the place. If I went alone, even with GPS, I'd probably get lost."

The trial I was preparing for involved a claim against a bank that had bounced a check it should have paid, resulting in my client losing a valuable contract for her business. This in turn started a domino effect which eventually led to her losing the business. The bank admitted it made a mistake in not paying the check, so the fight now was about causation and damages. If the check had been paid, would my client have secured the contract in question and, if so, would her business have made it through a subsequent economic rough patch, or would it have failed anyway? And what was the business – a travel agency – worth as a going concern? The bank's position is that the business was going down the tubes regardless and, even if it survived, its value as a going concern was far less than what we said it was. We'll be asking the jury for $600,000 in damages and had offered to take $450,000 in settlement. The bank had offered $25,000, leaving us no choice but to take the case to trial. My client was a widower whose husband had died of COVID during the pandemic, leaving her with two children to raise and a boatload of debt.

The trial, as usual in this type of case, would be heavy with expert witnesses, engaged to express opinions in support of the position whoever hired them was taking in the case. My expert, Marvin Lang, was one of the best around. He was a retired accountant who was a past president of the American Accounting Association and he was thoughtful, logical, sincere, honest, had a talent for explaining complicated things in an easy to understand manner and, to a jury, charming. He was not, like many others, an expert witness whore. If he didn't believe the opinions he was asked to give were correct, he would not accept the engagement. And he was always willing to discount his fees if a client of mine was in a circumstance of economic distress, which was certainly the situation here.

On Tuesday, after scrambling to get my work done, I made it to Maria's house at the appointed time of 4:00. The home was small – maybe 2,400 square feet. After Andy died, although she could have lived mansion-style with distributions from the Thurston Family Trust, Marie elected to downsize and simplify her life, including the disposition of rooms full of personal property she and Andy had accumulated during their marriage. The house had been built forty years ago when this neighborhood was first developed. The lot was almost an acre in size and had matured nicely with ponderosa and pinion pines, and cedar trees, native grasses and small islands of perennial flowers. The backyard was fenced on all sides and had become, as Maria had wanted, a refuge for wildlife trying to earn a living in what is commonly called in these parts the urban/wildlands interface. The National Forest was only a few blocks away and Maria's backyard was routinely visited by rabbits, feral cats, foxes, coyotes, racoons, wild turkeys, skunks, black bears, and an occasional mountain lion. It was also an annual stopover for migrating birds, including several species of hummingbirds, and grossbeaks, black-capped chickadees, nuthatches and eastern kingbirds, all of whom knew there would be a nice meal waiting for them when they stopped by for a visit. At the moment, the landscaping was showing signs of modest neglect. Some of the trees needed pruning. The flower beds still had the remnants of last year's plantings. The bird feeders were empty. But, at the time of my visit, there was a family of rabbits scampering around on the grass and grossbeaks were singing in the trees.

Going inside Maria's house was unsettling. I felt like a trespasser. I was surrounded by the souvenirs of someone else's life, someone who had just died. There were photos of Maria and Andy, including a few from their wedding day, and from various places they had visited and enjoyed. I recognized some of those places – Volcanoes National Park on the Big Island of Hawaii, Yosemite National Park, the Beaver Creek ski area, Asilomar Beach on the west side of the Monterey Bay peninsula. There was even a photo, from many years ago, of Maria and Andy with all three of the children – Duane, Billie, and Phillip – looking as though they were one big happy family.

Although Josie was long gone, her pooch pillow was still by the fireplace, along with one of her toys, which looked like a stuffed dragon. There was also jewelry in the bathroom, none with great economic value but all, no doubt, carrying memories of love and life. There were several nice paintings in the house, which I thought might in fact have economic value. One of the larger paintings was from Billie, and I found it attractive -- a colorful impressionist kind of mountain landscape. Scott would have to decide what to do with these items. Sell them? Give them to Phillip? Give them to a thrift store? Throw them in a dumpster? Maria didn't leave instructions for the disposition of her tangible personal property even though, on multiple occasions, Scott had urged her to do.

Scott and Shelley instructed me on the workings of the video camera and I dutifully recorded their movements through the house. This included a sound recording in which Scott explained what he was doing and what he was finding. This recording might get multiple plays when the litigation began and, all things considered, after reviewing the video, I concluded I had done reasonably well as a videographer.

We stayed at the house for maybe ninety minutes and then locked up and left.

Chapter 4

My trial began as scheduled on Wednesday, although we were nearly bumped from the docket by an emergency election law dispute that had been assigned to our judge, Roberta Parsons. However, Judge Parsons was able to convince the lawyers in that case to settle. She did this by suggesting to each of them, in private meetings, that they were likely to lose. (This is a technique judges sometimes use to move cases along.) After the settlement, the lights turned green for my case to proceed.

The first matter of business was jury selection. As usual, I was presented with a panel of prospective jurors who didn't want to be there and who had various backgrounds ranging from a Ph.D. in physics to an employee of a local sandwich shop. The jury selection system worked as designed, with the individuals each side most wanted on the jury being excused and the jurors who would finally decide the case having no particular expertise or experience in regard to the issues in dispute. But, in the end, I was confident the jurors selected were intelligent, could accurately process modestly technical information, were likely to stay awake during the trial, and would be thoughtful and fair. My prediction was that a school district administrator, Thomas Rasmusson, would end up as the jury foreman. In a jury trial, you always try to guess who the foreman will be and then focus on that individual as you present your case.

The lawyer representing the bank, Sam Chernek, was a good guy and a good lawyer. He was sure to represent his client well. However, I had something going for my side that he didn't – the fact that most people have had a bad experience with a bank and don't much like banks.

We presented our opening statements immediately after the noon recess. No surprises here. I told the jurors the evidence they would see and hear would convince them my client lost her business because of the bank's admitted error in not paying a check it should have paid and the business, which had a critical mass of loyal customers, would have been in a good position, after the pandemic, to recover, grow and prosper. Sam's pitch to the jury was that the contract my client was pursuing would have failed for a variety of reasons unrelated to the check the bank wrongfully bounced. And, even if that contract had been procured, my client would have lost her business anyway because the pandemic had shut down travel, meaning hard times for travel agencies.

After opening statements, it was my turn to present evidence. My first witness was my client, Cecilia Gomez, who told the jury about the creation and growth of her business, the importance of a contract with a major corporation to handle all its employees' travel needs, how that contract fell apart when the check she wrote to the corporation to establish a contingency reserve required by the contract had bounced, and how, when that contract failed, some of her other clients started bailing for fear her business could no longer meet their needs.

Sam, in a well-executed and understated cross examination, got Cecilia to admit that the pandemic had greatly and adversely affected the travel industry in general, and recovery had been slow. But Cecilia stood her ground and explained to the jury what she had done to reduce costs and that, after twenty years of good service, she had a core of regular clients who had stayed loyal and were counting on her to help them dig out of their own holes the pandemic had produced.

My expert witness, Marvin Lang, was then called. He did his usual good job explaining to the jury our position in the case. That is, the loss of the contract resulting from the bank's error had cut the legs out from under Cecilia's business and led to a nasty campaign of disparagement by other travel agencies eager to move in on Cecilia's client base. The consequence was a drop in revenue that left the business unable to cover its costs, and precipitated its failure. Marvin also told the jury that, if the important corporate employee travel contract had not been lost, Cecilia's business would have had the revenue it needed to march on through the pandemic and its regular client base would have remained intact. In that circumstance, the value of the business, based on the revenue it would have generated, would have been at least $600,000. The loss of that value was directly tied to the bank's mishandling of Cecilia's account. Marvin used cross examination, as a good expert witness will, to repeat and reinforce his direct testimony.

As my final witnesses, I called a couple of Cecilia's important long-term clients who told the jury they would have continued to patronize Cecelia's business if it hadn't been forced to shut down. Sam tried to get the judge to exclude this testimony as "character evidence" or speculation but that effort failed and the witnesses were allowed to say what I wanted them to say -- that Cecilia had been highly effective in meeting their travel needs for many years and they would have continued to be customers if the business had remained open.

The bank's expert witness, a woman who was a senior partner at a large multi-state accounting firm, was also very good. She augmented her testimony with charts and graphs showing what damage the pandemic had done to the travel industry. Her opinion testimony was that Cecilia's business was a goner, regardless of the contract Cecilia claims she lost because of the bank's error. On cross examination, however, I was able to get her to admit that the tide had turned; the travel industry was on the rebound; the past did not predict the future; and travel agencies that survived the hard times would be in an excellent position going forward because the number of competitors in the marketplace would have been reduced.

Sam called one other witness, a bank vice president in charge of checking account operations, who explained how a computer software malfunction, and not a careless bank employee, had caused the non-payment of the check Cecilia had written on her business account. My cross examination simply confirmed that the check should have been paid but was not, and the software that caused it to bounce was flawed and had since been modified to fix the problem.

We were now in a position to finish up the case on Friday, as anticipated, but after the noon recess, we again encountered a docket interruption. This time around it was a petition for a protective order filed by a woman who claimed her ex-boyfriend was stalking her. And, there was a request to reduce the bond of a teenage motorist who was in jail on a vehicular homicide charge and whose parents assured Judge Parsons their son would not be skipping out in an effort to avoid prosecution. Because of these interruptions, Judge Parsons sent the jury home at 2:00 p.m. with instructions to report back on Monday morning at 9:00 a.m. for closing arguments and deliberation. The judge told the jurors not to discuss the case with anyone over the weekend, including spouses, significant others, friends and pets. He ordered Sam and me to come back at 3:30 to work on the instructions the jurors would receive concerning the rules of law governing the case.

At our 3:30 meeting with Judge Parsons, as usual, the lawyers couldn't agree on all the jury instructions. I wanted an instruction telling the jury the bank was liable for all damages resulting from its wrongful refusal to pay Cecilia's check, including consequential damages. This means the bank's liability extended to all the dominoes that fell after the check was bounced, and not just the amount of the check. In other words, the loss of the business. Sam wanted an instruction telling the jurors they were not to consider character evidence -- good guy/bad guy evidence -- in reaching their verdict, and he disagreed with my wording on the instruction dealing with consequential -- all the dominoes -- damages. Jury instructions are important because they are meant to state, in simple terms, what the rules of law are that govern a case. And, not getting the instructions right is a ticket to the court of appeals for a party unhappy with the outcome of a trial. The reality is jurors don't really understand, and pay very little attention to, the instructions they receive.

Our meeting with the judge ended shortly after 4:30 and she said she would decide on the final content of the instructions before the jury came back on Monday. So, she said she would be ready to instruct the jury as a first item of business at that time and we should be prepared to present our closing arguments as soon as the instructions were given.

The jury would then move to the jury room and begin deliberations.

After we were dismissed by Judge Parsons, I stopped by the offices of Jensen & Kirkpatrick, which were between the courthouse and my office, to see if Scott was in and could give me an update on events associated with the death of Maria.

"Hi Melissa. Any chance Scott is in and could see me for a couple of minutes?"

"Hi Jack," said the long-time (and thoroughly charming) Jensen & Kirkpatrick receptionist. "Well, this may surprise you, but he's on the phone. However, I happen to know he's talking to another lawyer he doesn't much like so I expect the call to be short. Coffee? Soft drink?"

"No thanks. I'll just plop down in one of your overpriced Italian leather chairs, look out at Pikes Peak and see if I can wait him out. I was just heading back to my office from the courthouse and thought I'd take a chance on his being here."

While I waited for Scott, I fiddled around with my cell phone, most features of which are still a mystery to me. The financial markets had had another bad day thanks to trade problems with China and the lingering effects of the COVID pandemic, meaning my savings for retirement, meager to begin with, were again heading in the wrong direction. I also was able to check the baseball standings and was pleased to see the Rockies were no longer in the cellar of the National League West and had moved up to next to last. This was mostly because the Arizona Diamondbacks were in a rebuilding year and off to an even worse start than the Rockies.

Scott came out to the lobby ten minutes after my arrival, shook my hand and ushered us into one of the Jensen & Kirkpatrick expensively appointed conference rooms.

"So, Jack, how did the trial go?"

"Well, we won't know until Monday. We got pushed back by emergency hearings on a protective order petition – stalking by an ex-boyfriend -- and a criminal bond dispute, so we weren't able to finish up today. I thought we executed our game plan well but, as usual, anything can happen. Sam and his expert witness did a good job, as did Marvin Lang. This trial is the usual commercial litigation gambling event, but we had no choice but to roll the dice because of the unreasonable settlement offer made by the bank."

"I'm telling you Jack, you need a nice quiet 9 to 5 estate planning practice so you don't have to live your life as a professional gambler."

"Yeah, well, how are things going in your nice quiet 9 to 5 estate planning practice in connection with Maria Thurston's death and your duties as lawyer for her as trustee, personal representative for her estate, successor trustee, surrogate parent for a middle-aged irresponsible son of a dead person, and whatever else you are?"

"Not much new to report. Shelley is doing her usual great job of pushing through the barriers in the way of getting a handle on Maria's and the trust's assets, income and expenses, although one of Maria's banks is being a complete pain in the butt when it comes to accessing her accounts. So we can't as yet pay some of her bills. And I can also report that Duane has hired himself a Texas lawyer who has written me what I'm sure will be the first of many threatening letters. This letter basically says Duane is

planning to sue me and I need to be sure to preserve all
records in my possession and control having anything to do
with the trust's accounts and Maria's -- and my -- handling
of the Thurston Family Trust."

"Who's the lawyer?"

"His name is Carlton Jonas Manifort the third and
he's been around for a while. He was a partner at one of
Austin's more respected firms for a few years but they threw
him out -- or rather, strongly suggested he resign -- after a
bunch of ethical grievances, malpractice claims, and threats
of criminal prosecution for lobbying law violations and
sexual harassment. My contacts in my firm's Houston office
tell me he comes off as amiable but he can't be trusted to do
anything he says or pay any attention to the Rules of
Professional Conduct or the Rules of Civil Procedure."

"So what's next for me? By the way, I've given this
matter great thought and, solely out of respect and friendship
for you, although I have no idea where this is going to take
me and I fully expect to end up regretting my decision, I'm
accepting the engagement."

"Thanks. I'll do my best to be a respectful and
courteous client. As your first task, I'd like you to respond
to Mr. Manifort's letter, tell him you are my lawyer in
connection with all matters associated with the Thurston
Family Trust and Maria's estate, and he should communicate
only with you -- and leave me alone."

"OK. Email me a copy of his letter and I'll do my
duty. What happens after that?"

"We'll just have to see. I need to keep marching on
with the tasks that require prompt attention after someone
dies -- rounding up assets, paying bills, prudently investing
funds, spreading ashes. I'll ignore Duane and his lawyer

until I can't anymore. I do, however, have to engage with Phillip and nail him down to a budget. He's entitled to regular distributions out of the trust I'm now responsible for but only in amounts for reasonable expenses associated with his and his children's health, education and wellbeing and not for, say, first class plane fare to New Zealand for a vacation or a new Maserati. Andy kept Phillip on a short leash when he was alive, but when Andy died and Maria assumed the duties of trustee, Phillip learned to manipulate her into giving him a lot more of what he wanted. Now, as the trustee of this trust and having a duty running to all beneficiaries of the trust and the foundation, I can't be letting Phillip loot the trust estate for his own convenience and pleasure, or let Duane push me around under threat of being sued."

"Right. Sounds like a nice quiet 9 to 5 existence. I assume you get paid for this, right?"

"Well, I could but I won't. I won't be asking for fees for my work as trustee for this trust. Our firm will charge for the time of its staff but not mine. Maria was a friend, and Andy was a friend, and Maria has trusted me to carry out her last wishes. It wouldn't feel right to me to diminish the family's wealth by sticking my hand in the till. Maybe if I have to unscramble a complicated income tax conundrum down the road and I save the trust money by my efforts, I'll charge the trust something. Otherwise not."

"But you're going to pay me for my work, right?"

"Sure, but under your usual value-billing arrangement where your charges are based on the value you deliver to the client, if any, and not the amount of time you spend flailing around with the stuff that ends up on your desk."

"Right. That's how we do things at McConnel Jones & Knight, and those are the rules that apply here."

"Time for a drink?"

"Thanks Scott. But no. Veronica is coming down from Denver for the weekend and I'm in charge of tonight's dinner. She's had a long week since the Federal Reserve Board keeps comingling prudent management of the economy with politics."

Chapter 5

After my meeting with Scott, I stopped by my office briefly to make sure everything was under control, at least by my standards. My secretary, Stephanie, assured me it was. And, as usual, she told me things were more under control when I was out of the office than when I was in the office. When I got home, shortly after 5:00, Veronica's Subaru (sorely in need of a wash) was in my driveway and she was sitting on my front porch with Cooper, who continued to use Veronica every chance he got as another resource in pursuit of understanding women. Cooper was working on a Coors and Veronica had helped herself to a chardonnay.

Veronica Stailey and I had met several years ago when we ended up working together on a plot to blow up the U.S. economy by a group of radicalized scientists and social scientists who were convinced they had to act in order to get control of global warming and thereby save the planet. Veronica is a computer expert at the Fed and part of her work involves criminal investigations. My job in this matter had been to help Veronica investigate the death of an employee of my client, Front Street Bank, who had stumbled onto evidence of the plot and was thereafter murdered. The very sophisticated plan this group had developed involved taking over the Fed's computer network, Fedwire, that regulates the movement of money in the U.S., and globally. Then, after they had locked up most of the world's money, they intended to put in place a benevolent dictatorship run by scientists, which would save the earth from global warming, resolve issues of income inequality, prevent future pandemics, and otherwise make this a better world. The organization, which we called S.O.S. (short for Société Ombragée de Savants -- meaning in French "shadowy society of scientists"), was of the belief that governments, left to their own devices, would continue to make a mess of things and the human race would eventually face extinction as a consequence (and it's entirely possible they were right). Veronica and I, with the help of a large amount of luck, were able to shut down S.O.S.'s attack on the Fed's system just as it was about to launch. In the course of all this, Veronica and I, both carrying the scars of difficult divorces, had bonded and become more than just professional colleagues. We shared each other's company, and each other's beds, whenever possible. Veronica, who now lives in Denver, is a few years behind me in age, just turned fifty, and is a beautiful, sexy woman who is the bright spot in my life, with a higher rank even than fishing. Neither of us has had thoughts of marriage -- too scary to consider -- but we were compatible and comfortable in our relationship.

"Hi guys," I said, after parking my long-in-the-tooth fishing truck SUV next to Veronica's Subaru, and heading to the porch. "A nice evening to be outside. Have you solved any of Cooper's problems?"

"Hello Jack. Not yet but we're working on it, right Coop?"

"Hi Jack. Let me guess. It's time for me to surrender my beer can and head home."

"Cooper, I don't want to rush you or anything. But I'm sure your parents are worried about you and I promised Veronica I'd make dinner tonight. So, yes, it's time for you to head home."

And with that, Cooper put down his beer can, pouted his way off the porch and headed back to his parent's house, a block down the street, after which Veronica and I shared a long embrace.

"So, Veronica, how are things at the Fed?"

"Business, and politics, as usual. But we are dealing with a new S.O.S. flareup in Venezuela and I may be heading down there next week. It's not a great place to hang out these days but the work I need to do requires me to be there physically."

"Well, you can tell me more about it later, to the extent you're allowed to. Let's go inside before it gets chilly out here and let me go to work on grilled salmon and a salad."

"It sure is quiet without Fletcher. But, there's also less fur on the sofa."

"I miss that old dog. He's been gone six months now and the pain isn't going away. It was easier to lose my parents and my sister than to lose that dog."

Over dinner, Veronica told me more about the possible attack on the Venezuelan banking system which the Central Intelligence Agency had sniffed out with cell phone and email eves dropping. The situation was complicated for Veronica by the fact that the government of Venezuela was in disarray and getting cooperation from the government was next to impossible because the same people couldn't be counted on to be there two days in a row. I told Veronica about Scott's latest plunge into trust administration acrimony and let her know I considered her a part of the team to deal with whatever came of Duane's intent to blow up Maria's -- and now Scott's -- plans for the distribution of Andy's wealth. I also told her of my concerns that RJ's health was deteriorating.

After dinner, there was time for another glass of wine on the deck, watching the dark night sky come to life with Jupiter and Saturn hanging off the south side of Pikes Peak. And then it was early to bed for a nice snuggle, helping to chase away a week's worth of worries. As always, Veronica was warm (mostly -- there were a couple of cold spots) and soft, and smelled wonderfully of Shalimar, a new dose of which had been, I believe, applied for the occasion.

The next morning, I was up early and off to the office to put the final touches on my closing argument in the Cecilia Gomez trial. Veronica stayed at my house, consuming large quantities of tea and making plans for her trip to Venezuela, which was now looking like a definite go. She had to head back to Denver mid-afternoon to pack and load some new software into her industrial strength laptop. I made it home from my office just as she was putting her luggage (as usual, enough for a world cruise) into her car and getting ready to leave. We had a last kiss and hug, and she was off.

Since I was now ready for Monday's closing argument and a few final words with Judge Parsons about how she was likely to botch the jury instructions, I decided to head for the Arkansas River upstream from the Royal Gorge and see if the rainbow trout in the river were still in their feisty and hungry spawning season frame of mind. I was able to hook up with half a dozen small fish before the feeding suddenly shut down. But, the fish had no interest in my newly tied Adams 12 flies. They were grazing on emerging mayflies barely large enough to see.

Chapter 6

Monday morning, Judge Parsons refused to change her mind about the jury instructions and told Sam and me we each had only twenty minutes for our closing arguments. The judge said she had a busy criminal docket to plow through on Monday and she was already behind schedule since she had planned on our trial being completed last Friday.

Closing arguments produced no surprises. The jurors would either decide the bank's wrongful failure to pay Cecilia's check tanked her business and award her damages. Or they would decide the business was doomed no matter what because of the pandemic and not award damages.

The jurors were moved from the court room into the jury room to begin their deliberations at 9:40, and Sam and I were told to keep our cell phones on and be prepared for a quick trip back to the courthouse when the jurors completed their work. Cecilia took off to run a few errands and I went back to my office to wait, suffering the usual anxiety that comes when a trial is over and the jury is still out. Rebecca, Judge Parsons' clerk, called at 11:45 to say the deliberations were continuing but she thought we would have a verdict by 2:00, and she told Sam and me to be back in the courtroom at 2:00.

Judge Parsons brought the jurors back into the courtroom at 2:15. As is customary, everyone stood as the jurors came into the courtroom and retook their seats in the jury box. And, as usual, the jurors looked stern and refused to make eye contact with either Sam or me. I had guessed wrong about the foreperson. It was a woman who worked at an advertising agency, Jenelle Wilton, and not Thomas Rasmussen, the school district administrator. For no particular reason, I considered this a bad sign for my team.

"Do you have a verdict?" the judge asked.

"Yes, your honor, we do," Ms. Wilton responded.

"Very well. Please read the verdict."

"We, the jury, find for the plaintiff, Cecilia Gomez, and award her $600,000 in damages." A clear home run for my team. Cecilia started to cry and had to sit down. Sam and I shook hands, no words spoken. His client representative from the bank put on an unprofessional scowl and glared at the jurors.

The judge then discharged the jurors and thanked them for their service. She told them they were free to speak with the lawyers if they chose to do so, but they were under no obligation in that regard. Back in the jury room, I spoke briefly with Jenelle Wilton. She told me it took a while to get all members of the jury on board with a $600,000 verdict, but eventually Marvin Lang's expert testimony carried the day.

Outside the courthouse, Cecilia and I sat down on a bench in the shade of an elm tree that had just leafed out. She was still shaking from the stress of the trial and gushing thank you's at a rapid rate. After she calmed down a bit, I was able to explain to her what would happen next. I would get a call from Sam Chernek, who would tell me the bank intended to appeal the verdict based on an argument that the jury instructions were flawed. We would then have a negotiation wherein I would give modest weight to the threat of an appeal and the bank would give substantial weight to having to explain to its directors, regulators and shareholders why the bank's senior management had so badly underestimated the seriousness of Cecilia's claim. All of this would lead to a post-verdict settlement of maybe $550,000, enough for Cecilia to begin the task of rebuilding her business, and the litigation would be over. If there really was an appeal, the case would drag on for another two years and could possibly end up back in the trial court for a whole new trial in front of a whole new jury. From Cecilia's point of view, avoiding that scenario was clearly worth giving up $50,000.

After Cecilia had calmed down a bit and had headed home, I went back to my office to draft a letter to Carlton Jonas Manifort, Duane Thurston's Texas lawyer.

"Dear Mr. Manifort: This firm represents Scott Freeman in connection with the Thurston Family Trust and the estate of Maria Thurston. Please direct all further communications about these matters to me. Please also know that Mr. Freeman rejects all of your allegations that he has acted wrongfully in connection with his representation of Maria Thurston during her life and/or as the successor trustee of the Thurston Family Trust. Mr. Freeman further rejects your allegations that Maria Thurston had acted improperly in amending the trust agreement to change the manner in which the trust's assets would be distributed at her death. As I assume you know, Mr. Freeman is a highly professional, experienced and ethical estate planning and trust attorney. We will vigorously defend any attack on his actions, and on Maria Thurston's actions as trustee prior to her death.

"As you also presumably know, under Colorado law, which we believe controls in this situation, your clients, Duane and William Thurston, as named beneficiaries of the Thurston Family Trust, are entitled to certain information about the trust, notably its assets and liabilities, distributions the trust has made and modifications to the trust instrument. I will assemble that information and forward it to you. If you have questions after you receive this information, please let me know."

I wanted to add: "In the meantime, buzz off and cool your jets" but that would have been unprofessional so I closed the letter with "very truly yours, Jack McConnell," which sounded adequately hostile and condescending. I then sent an email to Scott attaching a draft of my letter to Manifort, asking him to approve the letter and to get to work rounding up the information Manifort was entitled to receive. Scott promptly approved the letter and I sent it to Manifort as an email attachment, and by regular mail.

Although late afternoons were outside my narrow window of enthusiasm for a trip to the Y and a workout, I decided that's what I should do to end my day. At the Y, I moved some weights around and tried to stretch out my 60-year-old, always stiff, muscles, took a shower, and decided I was due for a weigh-in. I was relieved to see I was holding onto my pre-50's and pre-60's weight of 175 pounds, and still measured six foot two inches on the scale's height measuring feature, notwithstanding early signs of deteriorating spinal disk disease, which seems to affect everyone over age 50 and makes you shorter. In general, all body parts continued to be functioning normally and I was looking forward to the start of the senior softball season, scheduled to begin in two weeks. I'd be playing in the over 60 league this year where, as one of the "younger" players, I might just have a chance at respectable performance. Although, when I first began playing with these guys (and a few ladies), there was just one league, for anyone over 50, now there's an over 50 league, an over 60 league and an over 70 league so, not unlike a life care assisted living facility, you could keep playing softball as you aged, at a level adjusted to your need for stronger pain meds.

When I got home, I checked my emails for news from Veronica. She was in Caracas, was staying at a nice and well protected hotel, had not been kidnapped or assaulted, and had hooked up with a team of government computer experts who seemed to be able to function in a manner unaffected by the political chaos Venezuela was experiencing. They were skilled and friendly and she looked forward to the collaboration. Veronica would be starting work with them in the morning in an effort to move in on the S.O.S.-inspired economic terrorists who were trying to take over the Venezuelan banking system and, hopefully, develop a strategy to shut this group down before it could strike and cause major damage.

Chapter 7

On Tuesday morning, I went for a jog around my neighborhood before breakfast. I said hello to the neighborhood dogs, all of whom knew me well. They showed no intention of aggression and generally ignored me or greeted me with a tail wag. When I made it to the office around 9:00, Scott's assistant, Shelley, had already delivered a package of the documents I had requested concerning the Thurston Family Trust and that I had concluded Manifort, as Duane's and Billie's lawyer, was entitled to see. I looked these over, found no surprises, and put them, along with a short cover letter, in a FedEx envelope for two-day delivery to Manifort.

Mid-morning, I received an email from Manifort saying he had received my letter of yesterday; he would talk to whoever he wanted to whenever he wanted to; Maria Thurston had no authority to change how the assets of the Thurston Family Trust were to be distributed; and Scott Freeman was a low life who had engaged in egregious acts of undue influence and should, among other things, have his license to practice law revoked. I forwarded the email to Scott and again resisted the temptation to tell Manifort, in an email reply, to cool his jets.

Scott sent me an "I told you so" response and asked if I would join him on Friday for a trip into Pike National Forest to break the law and spread Maria's and Andy's (and Josie's) ashes at the spot Maria had selected. Maria had instructed him, Scott told me, that there was to be no ceremony of any kind after her death, so none was planned.

I told him I would be honored to go with him and we arranged a departure time from his office of 2:00 p.m. Scott also told me that, in lieu of any kind of ceremony, he would be putting together a memorial booklet briefly telling the story of Maria's life and including photos of her and Andy. This would be sent to the few distant family members who had stayed in touch with Maria and a handful of other people whose names and addresses Scott had found in Maria's computer. She was a very private person and her contacts list was small.

Friday turned out to be a perfect day for a hike into Pike National Forest, starting from a residential neighborhood that lies just to the west of the Garden of the Gods. I was very familiar with the trail we would be on and knew that it was, in parts, steep and rocky. I therefore brought along a set of trekking poles for Scott, worried that he wasn't in the best of shape for this kind of outing.

The spot Maria had picked for Andy and her (and Josie) to spend eternity was magnificent. It sat along a ridge that, to the west, dropped off precipitously into Williams Canyon and offered an unobstructed view of the northeast face of Pikes Peak. There was still abundant snow in the couloirs that run down this side of the mountain and that, in my youth (and goaded on by thrill seeking irresponsible friends), I had occasionally descended on skis.

Scott did OK on our hike, which was no more than a mile, although he required occasional stops to replenish oxygen. When we arrived at the location for the ashes to be spread, we sat down on a rock outcropping and enjoyed the view and tranquility, and our friendship. I had brought along a bottle of California pinot noir for the occasion, from my small collection of upscale wines saved for special events, and we shared that while we talked about Maria and Andy, and life and death. Scott, as an estate planning lawyer, dealt with death on a daily basis. It was, after all, his job to help people deal with the economic issues associated with death. But, this inevitably brought him in contact with the intimate thoughts and fears of his clients going far beyond what might happen to their assets and liabilities when they died, or taxes.

"So Scott," I asked after a second glass of wine, "are you afraid of death?"

"McConnell, no I'm not afraid of death. I consider it an inconvenience that must be dealt with like many other things. People have been dying for tens of thousands of years, and none of them seem to be complaining about it after they die. So, when my time comes, I am confident I will muddle through death to a successful conclusion. Plus, they have good drugs these days to take pain out of the equation. I'm not big on pain. What about you, and do you have any more wine?"

"No more wine. I still need to get you back down the trail in one piece. Well, I try not to think about death. I'm counting on people like you -- in fact you precisely -- to help me die in an orderly fashion so I won't leave legal chaos as my legacy. As you know, since you did my will, I have no close blood relatives and when I die my wealth, such as it is, is going to Trout Unlimited. I may decide to give Cooper a little money to help him get started in life, and a little money to Veronica to remind her that I love her, but that's about it. You're getting my collection of 19th century America literature. Oh, and a signed copy of one of John Grisham's novels. I met him at a book signing in Denver a couple of years ago."

It was then time to attend to the task at hand. Scott opened the sealed bags that contained the ashes of Maria and Andy and Josie. He gave me one of the bags and kept the other two, and we then scattered the ashes along the ridge. I was again surprised that the ashes of a human body, after cremation, would take up so little space -- not much more than Josie. A sudden, and cold, wind coming down off Pikes Peak assisted us in spreading the ashes and the whole process took less than two minutes. It was then time to hike back down the trail and head home. Scott slipped once on the scree but caught himself with help from the trekking poles and no damage was done.

Chapter 8

On Monday, Manifort, having apparently decided to start the legal warfare as quickly as possible, had a process server pay Scott a visit at his office and hand to him a summons and complaint, meaning the start of a lawsuit. The lawsuit had been filed in a state court in Texas. Manifort could do this because the Thurston Family Trust had been created by Andy while he was still a resident of Texas and before he and Maria moved to Colorado. The plaintiffs in the lawsuit were Duane and William Thurston. The only defendant was Scott.

The complaint claimed that Scott had, through improper means -- the legal term is undue influence -- coerced Maria into changing how the trust's assets were to be distributed after her death -- Duane's and Billie's haircut. It accused Scott of breach of fiduciary duty and fraud. Manifort's evil strategy behind the fraud claim was that Scott's malpractice insurance would not cover a claim for fraud because fraud is an intentional legal wrong. So, Scott's personal assets would now be put at risk -- his home, cars, retirement savings, ownership interest in his law firm, money he'd saved for his grandchildren's college education, etc. This was, bottom line, the legal equivalent of knee kicking -- as nasty as it gets. The complaint asked that Duane's and Billie's interest in the trust be restored to what it was before Maria changed it, sought to hold Scott personally responsible for the amount taken away from Duane and Billie -- many millions of dollars -- and asked the court to make Scott responsible for the attorney's fees Manifort would wrack up in the litigation.

Scott sent a copy of the complaint to me by email, without comment. I gave it a quick review and called him on the phone.

"Well, Scott, you were right. Duane wants to play hardball. I'll work on an answer to the complaint, and a counterclaim for abuse of process -- that is, filing a lawsuit without real substance and as a means of personal attack. This will be a hard claim to prove, but it will at least give Duane something to think about. As you know, we'll need a Texas lawyer to join in your representation since I'm not licensed in Texas -- and don't want to be. Maybe your firm, through its Houston office, can recommend someone. I don't want to use a lawyer from your firm. Better to have someone who has no connection to you. The Texas lawyer won't have to do much other than to make sure we comply with Texas court rules. But, he or she might be a source of helpful information about our judge and Manifort, and also quirks of Texas law. In the meantime, you need to notify your firm, and your firm's malpractice insurer, that you've been sued. Your firm is a big enough player on the malpractice insurance stage that you, and not the insurance company, should have the right to name the lawyer who will defend the claims against you, so hopefully it will let me be your lawyer, even though it's never heard of me."

"Jack, filing the lawsuit isn't all that Duane Thurston has done. He has also filed a grievance with the Colorado Supreme Court claiming I have violated the Colorado Rules of Professional Conduct and should have my law license revoked."

"More dirty tricks. Most of those claims get thrown out early on, but we'll deal with that and try to keep you out of harm's way. Send me a copy of the correspondence you've received about this filing."

"I hope you know this is not fun. I have been a careful, ethical, caring lawyer devoted to the best interests of my clients for thirty plus years now, and it's a punch in the gut to be accused of fraud and violations of fiduciary duties and violations of the Rules of Professional Conduct."

"You'll be OK Scott. As you know, the legal system has warts but, by and large, it scratches its way to the truth, is not easily manipulated by people who want to use it to harm other people, and mostly works in the way we grew up believing in. Go home. Have a martini, or better, a glass of merlot, watch the Rockies game, and we'll regroup tomorrow. Your duties going forward are to ignore all this background noise and act responsibly as Maria's personal representative, the successor trustee of the Thurston Family Trust and, soon, the CEO of the Thurston Family Foundation."

"Thanks Jack. I can't believe how thin skinned I seem to be about all this. I'm glad you're on my team. And grateful to have you as a friend as well as my lawyer."

My personal thoughts were, of course, less optimistic than what I had conveyed to Scott. The legal system is capable of all manner of atrocities meaning, in this case, Scott could end up liable for damages that could wipe out his entire net worth and he could have his license to practice law suspended or revoked. Unlikely, yes. But impossible, no.

The next day, I had my expected telephonic negotiation with Sam Chernek intended to bring finality to

Cecelia Gomez's lawsuit. After a couple of rounds of lawyer posturing wherein Sam threatened an appeal and I told him his appeal would go nowhere, would last for years and would require his client to provide bank regulators and the bank's directors with all manner of information on a monthly basis, we agreed that the bank would promptly pay Cecilia $550,000 and there would be no appeal. Cecilia was happy with this result and was already well on her way to reopening her business. Sam agreed to prepare the necessary paperwork and obtain a cashier's check for the settlement amount.

Later in the day, I spoke with Scott. Understandably, he was stressed by Duane Thurston's attack on his honesty and integrity, was having trouble concentrating on his legal work, and hadn't slept all night. We discussed the fact that he was now shut down from distributing the bulk of the assets of the Thurston Family Trust to the Thurston Family Foundation, as he believed he was required to do as a fiduciary under the trust agreement. This couldn't be done until the litigation was concluded. In the meantime, he would have to prudently invest the trust's assets to avoid further legal bullets coming from Duane.

Scott's firm's Houston office had provided us with the name of a highly regarded Austin lawyer for us to use as our Texas attorney. Her name was Sylvia Everson, a seasoned trial attorney with a small boutique litigation firm. University of Texas law degree. A decade of experience with a big Texas firm before deciding small is better than big.

I called Sylvia shortly after I had spoken with Scott, and got right through to her, a rarity in this business. I told her what was going on and, after our call, emailed her a copy of the complaint filed against Scott. She called me back toward the end of the day and said she had no conflicts to worry about and she would be glad to serve as our local Texas counsel. She said she knew the judge, Brian Elefson, to whom this case had been assigned and he was a mixed bag. Reasonably bright and hardworking, but political, maneuvering to get himself appointed as a Federal district court judge, meaning a lifetime appointment. Elefson was better at criminal law than civil law, Silvia said, and, to her knowledge, he had no real experience in trust or probate law. She also confirmed what we had previously heard about Manifort -- pleasant to talk to but not to be trusted and no respect for rules of procedure or ethics. Sylvia said she would send me an engagement letter, confirming her position as local Texas attorney for Scott Freeman.

The next morning, at around 11:00, as I was heading out from my office for a trip to the Y for an aging body parts workout, I received a call from Heidi Freeman (no relation to Scott), the veterinarian who had tended to Fletcher's needs during his life and had helped, with a house call, to put him down when the time came.

"Hi Jack. How are you? Listen, I have a situation on my hands that made me think of you. A couple of clients of mine were killed last week in a horrible car accident on I-25 on their way north to see friends. They have left behind a three-year old Golden retriever named Elsie, who is now an orphan. A neighbor, who had a key to the house, brought Elsie to me and she is staying with me here at the clinic. Elsie's guardians had no kids and no other close relatives. Apparently, there's a sister who lives in British Columbia but that's it. I need to find Elsie a home and, well, I thought of you. Elsie is a sweetheart of a dog. She's used to being a single dog, loves everyone and every other dog. She's housebroken and has been content to spend her days lying around on her dog bed while her guardians are away. But she'll chase a tennis ball with enthusiasm when given the opportunity. She's trained on and off leash on basic commands – come, sit, stay, dinner. She came from a careful breeder and has no health issues we know of. So, I was thinking maybe she'd be a good dog for you to fill the gap in your life caused by the passing of Fletcher. In any event, I was hoping you might have time to stop by the clinic and meet Elsie, and see what you think. Can you do that?"

"Oh Heidi, I've just gotten used to being dogless and I have started to enjoy not spending my weekends picking up poop and vacuuming up dog hair."

"Well, maybe you could just foster her for a couple of weeks and see how it goes. That would really help me. Our clinic is not set up for long term borders and we're full of animals in recovery from surgeries at the moment."

"OK, fine. As a favor to you, I'll stop by late this afternoon, at around 4:30. Will that work?"

"Yes. I'll be here, and so will Elsie. Thanks."

Heidi's clinic, All Creatures Animal Care, was on my way home anyway and I pulled into the parking lot shortly after 4:30. Heidi met me at the door and gave me a hug. She asked me to wait in the lobby and then she brought out Elsie on a leash. Elsie had a reddish-brown coat which, Heidi said, was typical of a lineage bred for hunting, although Elsie had never been a hunting dog. She had big soulful brown eyes and a feathery tail, which she was gently wagging. She came up to me, went into a sit without a command to do so, looked at me, and gently licked my hand.

"So Heidi, how many fostered dogs that you have processed over the years ever came back to you?"

"Well, let's see. I can think of one. A Russel terrier named Dino who destroyed two sofas and a coffee table in a matter of minutes. I'm sure there have been others but I don't remember them just now."

"Two weeks. I'll take Elsie home with me for two weeks. That's it, and that will give you time to look for a permanent home for her."

"Thanks Jack. That will really help me out. Let me get her dog bed and a couple of days of the food she has been eating, and you can be on your way."

"Don't I, like, have to sign some kind of contract?"

"Oh, maybe later. Let's not worry about that today."

So Heidi and I helped Elsie, and her dog bed, into the back seat of my SUV and headed to my place. I needed to coax her out of the car after we pulled into my driveway, but she then went into a full court sniffing tour of my front yard, where she no doubt still found scents of Fletcher even though he had been gone for many months. She chose a few places to mark as her own, followed me into the house with a single "come" command, and began another olfactory exploration, this time of all the places Fletcher used to hang out in my house. I gave her her dinner and water in Fletcher's old bowls and she seemed happy with that. She then settled into her dog bed, which I had placed on top of Fletcher's old dog bed, while I made myself a microwave dinner and turned on the Rockies game. At around 8:30, I took Elsie out for a nature call and brought her dog bed into my bedroom. We then tucked ourselves in for a quiet night.

In the morning, I gave Elsie her breakfast and introduced her to my backyard, which was fenced. While

Elsie explored the backyard, I took a shower, put on my lawyer uniform of the day (khaki pants, a blue button-down collar shirt -- most buttons intact -- and a tie with multiple images of trout flies). I brought Elsie back in the house, told her to be a good girl and headed to my office. I went back home at noon and checked on her. She was fine, curled up on her dog bed. She gave me a wag and a lick, and a look that said thank you, and then accepted an invitation to revisit the backyard.

By the time I got back home late afternoon, it was already clear to me that Elsie was here to stay; she was not going back to Heidi. My dogless days were over and the next chapter of my-life-as-a-series-of-dogs had begun. I sent Veronica an email, with pictures of Elsie, and told her what had come to pass. She responded with approval, said her mission in Venezuela was winding up, and she was eager to get back home and meet Elsie, as long as Elsie had not taken over her place in my bed.

In the morning, I called Heidi and told her to prepare the adoption paperwork and accused her of tricking me with the old foster care bait and switch routine. I also pulled up chewy.com on my laptop and ordered a two-month supply of the dog food Heidi had given me.

For the rest of the week, I took Elsie out for a walk around my neighborhood each evening when I came home from work. She was great on a leash, immediately and without a command went into a sit every time a car went by, and wasn't nearly as devoted as Fletcher had been to claiming every square inch of our neighborhood as her territory.

On our walks, we ran into several of my neighbors, and several of my neighbors' dogs, most of which are the kind you can pick up and carry home with you if they misbehave. Elsie was a perfect lady during these encounters. Although I still missed Fletcher, this was a decided improvement in canine behavior since Fletcher, whenever we crossed paths with another person -- especially a person with a dog -- would immediately bolt out of a heel command at warp speed and go say hello, resulting in occasional injuries to my shoulder. Fletcher would demand a head scratch from the person we had encountered, and a shared butt sniff with the other dog, before we could continue our walk.

Elsie and I continued our new shared life over the next week. Cooper stopped by for a visit during that time and was introduced to Elsie. They were immediately pals and I came home one evening to find them sitting on my front porch, side by side and with Elsie's head in Cooper's lap. Cooper had a beer from my refrigerator. Elsie had a tennis ball from Fletcher's collection.

Veronica made it home from Venezuela toward the end of the week and came immediately to Colorado Springs from Denver International Airport, not stopping at her condominium in LoDo. She looked exhausted, but still beautiful. She and Elsie hit it off at first wag, and Elsie followed Veronica around the rest of the evening, until bedtime, when the bedroom door was closed long enough for a welcome back snuggle. We then took Elsie out for a last chance to pee on the crabapple tree in my front yard and invited her back into the bedroom, where she promptly settled into her dog bed and slept peacefully through the night.

Veronica and I spend Saturday catching up, and going for a long bike ride. The Venezuela situation was under control since Veronica and her Venezuelan colleagues had been able to put a sophisticated computer firewall in place around Venezuela's banking system network that would fend off any attack by S.O.S. We grilled halibut on the deck for dinner and ate outside, with Elsie at our feet.

Sunday, I left Veronica and Elsie to fend for themselves and headed to the South Platte River, where the rainbows, as the water warmed, were sipping tiny mayflies but still had no interest in an Adams 12.

Chapter 9

On Monday, after a triage of the week's work, I called Scott to see how he was doing and to tell him Manifort wanted to take his deposition, and wanted him to come to Texas for that event. Whether Scott could be compelled to travel to Texas for a deposition was one of those things lawyers could fight about at great length, and at great expense to their clients. In any event, I told Scott I would tell Manifort no, you are not going to Texas for a deposition. If Manifort wants to burn some of his client's cash and present the issue to Judge Elefson, he can do so, but his chances of success would be slim to none and he's an experienced enough lawyer to know that.

What we will offer Manifort, I said, is a virtual deposition, where Scott will stay here in Colorado, with a court reporter and a videographer in the room. Manifort, unless he wanted to spend a few days in Colorado, would participate with a Zoom connection. That would allow him to have a second video record of the deposition, compliments of Zoom. Scott agreed to this and, after a predictable professional pout, so did Manifort. We agreed the deposition would take place three weeks down the road, with Scott, the court reporter, the videographer, and me located in a conference room at Scott's office. Manifort, since it was already getting hot in Texas and/or tornadoes were already in the forecast, eventually decided a few days in Colorado sounded good and he would attend the deposition in person.

"Jack," Scott said to me after we worked through the deposition scheduling issues, "I'm not doing well as the defendant in a lawsuit, and the respondent in a Supreme Court grievance. I'm even more irritable than usual and I'm not sleeping worth a damn. Any suggestions?"

"I think you should have a visit with Rollie Dumbarton, our doctor, and see if he can recommend some stress relieving meds, other than martinis. My advice, as you know, is that you take up fly fishing as a calming activity. But we've had this conversation many times before and you have always rejected by advice. As I recall, your comment has consistently been something to the effect that standing around in cold water on slippery rocks, with a life-threatening current rushing by, with the intent to inflict pain on a beautiful innocent aquatic animal such as a trout, and risking skin cancer from sunburn, held no appeal to you."

"Correct. Martinis involve none of those hazards."

"OK, well, firm up a date on your calendar for this deposition and reserve one of your plush conference rooms. Let's get this over with. I know you've taken, and otherwise participated in, lots of depositions during your career but I will nonetheless get with your assistant Shelley and schedule time with you to go over what you are going to be asked and how you might wish to respond."

With one exception, the rest of the week proved to be routine, including evening walks around my neighborhood with Elsie. The exception was a visit to RJ, finally back from his winter in Arizona. RJ taught me most of what I know about trying a lawsuit and everything I know about catching trout with a fly rod. He's now 80 years old and, for the last several years, has been spending his winters at a little low-cost campground near Tucson, living out of his vintage Winnebago recreational vehicle (zero to sixty in 30 minutes). His regular home, in Manitou Springs, was built maybe 90 years ago and, as best I can tell, still has its original windows, siding, paint and plumbing. At some point, the roof must have been replaced thanks to one of the many hailstorms that sweep through this part of the world. But, the roof was looking like it could do with a freshening as well.

RJ and I would always plan a fall fishing trip into the Colorado high country in pursuit of late season trout, but that tradition ended last year because of RJ's various age-related infirmities. While RJ is in Arizona, I try to stop by his house once a week to be sure everything is OK. RJ's return from Arizona was a few weeks later than usual this year, and it was time for me to check in with him.

RJ was on his porch when I arrived, in his favorite old chair. I brought Elsie along so RJ could meet her. Elsie immediately ran up to RJ and gave him a lick, and then went into canine play mode with RJ's constant companion, Abbey, an Australian shepherd mix. Abbey was now an elder dog and could no longer provide Elsie with the same enthusiasm she had shown when Fletcher paid her a visit. Elsie quickly realized this and the two dogs settled in on the porch, next to RJ's feet. RJ was well into his evening dose of Jack Daniels when we arrived and offered me an opportunity to share. I went into the kitchen, which was a complete mess, poured myself a small drink and returned to the porch.

"RJ, welcome back to Colorado. Other than for the family of racoons living in your woodshed, your house has had a quiet winter. How are you holding up?"

"It's been a hard winter, Jack. The arthritis in my hands has made it impossible to even button a shirt. And there's no way I will ever again be able to tie a fly or even put a fly on the end of a tippet. Plus, my eyes are shot and my hearing is shot and I have a pinched nerve in my lumbar spine which makes it painful to walk. And modern medicine has nothing to offer me for any of this except nonstop appointments and big bills. My days consist of visiting doctors and sitting on the porch here, missing my wife, who has now been gone four years, watching the tourists go by, and trying not to pour the Jack Daniels until the sun starts to set behind Pikes Peak. I'd always hoped to leave a little money when I died to help my kids and my grandkids. But now it looks like the medical profession will suck up all that's left of my savings from a lifetime of work. Whatever."

"RJ, I'm sorry to hear all that. Hopefully, you'll be feeling better when it warms up and we can at least make a trip to one of the local reservoirs where we can fish from the bank, without having to walk too far or wade. And I can still see well enough to tie a fly onto your tippet. How are your kids doing?"

"They're still both in Denver and come down to see me every once in a while. But, you know, they're busy with their own lives and trying to raise their own kids -- two each. So, they don't have much time for me."

"And how is the Winnebago doing?"

"It's got its own issues with old age. It needs new tires and shocks and the radio quit working on my way back from Arizona. I suppose it's time to look for another vehicle and give this one to some charity, which can auction it off for scrap. But, frankly, I can't afford to buy another vehicle."

"I'll keep my eye out for something that will work for you. I have a couple of used car dealer clients and they'll know how to find just what you need. We'll get you fixed up. Hey, keep Elsie company here for a few minutes. I'm going to go inside and tidy things up a bit."

"You don't have to do that. I can take care of those things myself."

"That's OK RJ. I don't mind. Glad to help out. And next time, I'll bring Veronica along. She's a whizz at straightening things up and you and I can then stay on the porch and talk about fishing."

Straightening things up was a considerable understatement. I started by throwing clothes, sheets and towels in the washing machine and then tackling the kitchen. Next was the refrigerator, the contents of which went back to before RJ had left for Arizona, and probably earlier than that, and constituted a public health hazard. I loaded the items most in need of discard into a heavy-duty trash bag, which I would then take home and dispose of as part of my own household garbage.

After an hour of this, I went back to the porch and found RJ asleep in his chair. I woke him up, took him and Abby back into the house, made him some canned spaghetti for dinner, gave Abby her dinner of dry dog food, put Elsie back in my SUV and headed home, worried about what I could do to keep RJ safe -- and having no good ideas. RJ would never agree to move to an assisted living facility and, even if he was willing, he didn't have the money to do so. I decided the best thing I could do was contact his children in Denver and try to get them further engaged in helping their father. I called them the following day and they assured me they would find time for a trip down to Manitou Springs to visit RJ and work on a plan for his needs that he, and they, could afford.

Chapter 10

After we settled on a date for Scott's deposition, I met with him at his office to go over what was likely to come up during the deposition. As noted, although Scott had been involved in many depositions during his career as a lawyer, he had never actually been the deponent. And, as might be expected, he had noticeable anxiety about being placed under oath and asked questions about his and a client's affairs, with his answers to be recorded both on video equipment and transcribed by a court reporter, and likely to be used against him in a trial.

"Scott, you know the usual advice we give clients before a deposition. Answer the questions truthfully and succinctly, but don't volunteer information unless we decide there would be a good tactical reason to do so. Here, there might be, but we won't call that shot until we see what has come of Manifort's questioning. Before the deposition, you should go over your time records and billing statements showing the work you did for both Andy and Maria, to get the chronology down."

"Right. I've already rounded up those documents and had my secretary make a list of all the files we created. Which raises a big question for me about attorney-client privilege. Am I correct that the attorney-client privilege is owned by the client and not the lawyer, and survives death? Therefore, can someone in my position, as the successor trustee for the Thurston Family Trust and a lawyer who did legal work for both Andy and Maria, and who is now handling Maria's estate, assert the attorney-client privilege on their behalf and refuse to answer questions about communications I had with them?"

"This gets tricky. You are correct that the privilege is owned by the client and not the lawyer. But you are not entirely correct that the privilege survives death. Control of the privilege transfers to a decedent's personal representative and the personal representative can either assert it or waive it and will often waive it because the personal representative wants information from the lawyer in order to administer the estate. In any event, at the first level of analysis, a lawyer should not -- and ethically cannot -- testify about things a client said to the lawyer, even though the client is dead. So you are certainly in a position to refuse to answer questions about communications you had with Maria and Andy. But, here's what I think we should do. We should try to cut a deal with Manifort whereby you agree that Maria and Andy have, one way or another, waived the attorney-client privilege and Manifort in turn agrees to waive the hearsay rule. That rule would also come into play in this situation, since your communications with Maria and Andy would be hearsay -- that is, out of court statements not made under oath. If we do this deal with Manifort, all your communications, both oral and in writing, with Andy and Maria could come into evidence. And frankly, I like the idea of a jury having access to all that information. You can tell the jury, using Maria's own words, why Duane's and Billie's interests in the trust were cut back -- because she thought Duane was a jerk, dragging his brother Billie along in pursuit of no good, and that Andy, if he were still alive, would not want his wealth to move in their direction. Rather, once Maria died, he would want the Thurston Family Foundation to be created, as called for in the trust instrument, and the Foundation to get most of the money now in the trust."

"So, basically, we just let everything hang out, is that your proposal?"

"Yes. Manifort is going to try to convince the jury that you manipulated Maria and coached her into cutting back what Duane and Billie would get out of the trust when she died. You did this, he will argue, because you would then have a nice book of legal work going on for years to come involving the establishment and operation of a large charitable foundation and also the ongoing supervision of what Phillip would be allowed to do with the money he pulls out of the trust."

"Jack, that's ridiculous."

"Well, as you know, juries sometimes buy into ridiculous theories of human behavior. And, since jurors don't much like lawyers to begin with, a jury in this case could take out its hostility toward lawyers on you, nice guy that you are. 'Greedy lawyer manipulates aging client to change late husband's inheritance instructions in order to generate fees.' So, I say, let's let the jurors hear, in her own words, why Maria did what she did. You can be cross examined, but not Maria, since she's dead."

"So, whatever Manifort asks me about my client relationships and communications with Andy and Maria I should answer, while you sit on your butt and not object?

"Correct."

"Well, I want to think about that. Any other advice for me?"

"No. Except that, even though it's not your style, try to relax -- and stop trying to be your own lawyer."

Chapter 11

Scott's deposition occurred on schedule, in a mid-size conference room at the offices of Jensen & Kirkpatrick. The court reporter hired by Manifort for the event was there, along with the videographer he had hired, and they already looked bored. Scott of course was there, as was I. Manifort showed up 20 minutes late, but at least he had the courtesy to call and tell us he was behind schedule due to some client emergency back in Texas he was trying to manage long distance. I thought Duane might decide to attend. However, he did not.

Manifort, when he finally arrived, was wearing jeans and a leather vest, over a dark blue pinpoint cotton shirt with the top two buttons undone, and pointy-toed cowboy boots. He had a gold chain around his neck and spoke with a modest southern accent. Pretty much what I expected from a Texas lawyer. But, he was pleasant enough.

Before the deposition began, I pitched him on the idea that Scott would take the position that Andy and Maria, or their personal representatives, had knowingly waived the attorney-client privilege if he, Manifort, would waive hearsay objections. He didn't seem to have given much thought to any of this but, since he wanted to fish around for statements from Maria and Andy that would be of use to him, he agreed to my proposal. So, when the deposition began, the first thing I did was put our agreement on the record. Then, it was Manifort's turn to begin the questioning.

He started out with the usual questions about Scott's education and experience, and the kind of law he practiced. He then moved on to questions about how Scott came to represent first Andy and then Maria. And after that, he moved on to the meat of the matter.

"Am I correct, Mr. Freeman, that you are the lawyer who drafted the trust agreement for the Thurston Family Trust"

"Yes, that's correct."

"And that document, as originally written, said the trust, if Andy was the first to die, would first see to the needs of Maria and then at her death, Duane and William and Phillip would each get 10% of the trust's assets?"

"Yes, that's mostly correct. At Andy's death, and assuming Maria survived him, each of the three children were to receive PharmOne stock having a value of $3 million, which they did. Then, the balance of the assets in the trust would be dedicated to the health and welfare of Maria. At the death of Maria, assuming she was the last to die, each of the children – Duane, Billie and Phillip – would receive 10% of the trust's value at that time, in PharmOne stock. The balance of the assets in the trust would go into a newly created charitable foundation, to be called the Thurston Family Foundation."

"But that go changed, right?"

"Correct. Approximately fifteen months after Andy's death, Maria amended the trust instrument to reduce the amount that, at her death, would go to Duane and Billie. Under this amendment, at Maria's death, they would each receive 1% of the value of the trust in PharmOne stock, roughly $3 million. Phillip would still receive 10% of the value of the trust in PharmOne stock, roughly $30 million, although a good part of that would be restricted to uses benefiting Phillip's two children – Maria's grandchildren. The balance of the trust's assets -- 88%, roughly $255 million -- would go into the new, to be created, charitable foundation, the Thurston Family Foundation."

"So, when this amendment to the trust instrument was made, were you representing Maria and, if so, were you representing her personally or in her capacity as the successor trustee of the Thurston Family Trust?"

"Both. I was representing Maria as the successor trustee of the Thurston Family Trust and I was representing her individually as a beneficiary of the trust, and as someone who needed to have her own estate plan in place."

"OK, did she ask you whether, as the successor trustee of the trust, she could change its terms?"

"Yes."

"And what did you tell her?"

"I told her that, as the successor trustee of the trust after Andy's death, she could change how the trust's assets would be distributed at her death in any manner she chose, within the bounds of the trust's essential purposes."

"And what were the trust's essential purposes?"

"According to the trust instrument, they were to be sure Maria's needs were met during her lifetime and, at her death, that Duane, Billie and Phillip would each receive a discretionary gift, and the Thurston Family Foundation would be created for the purpose of supporting cutting edge pharmaceutical research and receive the remaining assets."

"Did Maria ask you how much discretion she had in making a gift to Duane, William and Phillip?"

"Yes."

"And what did you tell her?"

"I told her the trust instrument did not limit her discretion."

"Is that still your opinion?"

"Yes."

"Is it your opinion that no other limits applied to her discretion?"

"Correct."

"So Maria, in her position as successor trustee after Andy's death, instructs you to prepare an amendment to the trust instrument, right? And does she tell you the gifts to Duane and William, at her death, are to be greatly reduced?"

"Yes."

"Does she ask your advice about this?"

"Yes and no. She had made up her mind about reducing the amount Duane and Billie would receive, and she did not ask for my advice about that. She only wanted to know from me if, as successor trustee to Andy, she could make these reductions."

"And what did you tell her?"

"As I said, in my opinion, she could."

"So who in all this was representing the trust?"

"The trust, as you probably know, has no separate legal existence. It's not like a corporation or a limited liability company, which have a separate legal identity. In the case of a trust, all rights and obligations reside in the trustee. Although Colorado, at least, allows real estate to be titled in the name of a trust as though it was a separate legal entity, in some states, and Texas may be one of them, even real estate assets of a trust, and all personal property, must be titled in the name of the trustee. In any event, the answer to your question is that the trust, which has no status as a separate legal entity, did not have a lawyer. The trustee had a lawyer. After Andy's death, Maria was the successor trustee and I was her lawyer when she was wearing that hat."

"Well, did you tell Maria she needed to notify Duane and William in advance of her decision to amend the trust agreement?"

"No."

"Why not?"

"Because she had no obligation to do that. Duane and Billie, as beneficiaries, have no right to meddle in the trustee's decision making. If they don't like a decision the trustee makes, their recourse is to sue the trustee for breach of a trustee duty. They didn't do that and there's now a question whether they still can, or whether any such claim is barred by a statute of limitation. Instead, now that Maria is dead, your clients have chosen to sue me and I don't believe I had any legal duty owing to them at the time Maria chose to amend the trust agreement."

"Well how are Duane and William supposed to challenge Maria's amendment of the trust agreement within some applicable statute of limitations period if they never knew about the amendment?"

"That's a question for you to answer, Mr. Manifort. My position, as I stated, is that Maria had no duty to tell beneficiaries of the trust that she had exercised the power given her to amend the trust agreement."

"Are you saying that you, as the lawyer representing the trustee and therefore the trust, have no duties owing to the beneficiaries of the trust?"

"No. I'm saying I had no duty to the beneficiaries at the time Maria decided to amend the trust agreement to inform them of Maria's decision. I now have a duty to the beneficiaries as the successor trustee and that duty is to administer the trust in accordance with the trust agreement's terms, as amended, which is what I am doing."

"OK, so who do you think Duane and William can sue to challenge Maria's decision to hijack their inheritance?"

"First, it's not an inheritance. They are named beneficiaries of a trust, subject to the powers of a successor trustee to change the terms of the trust instrument. And as to who they can sue, I'm not going to give legal advice to your clients. My position is that they can't rightfully sue me."

"Assuming we decide to file a claim against Maria's estate, who is her personal representative?"

"Mr. Manifort, you're ahead of the game. Maria just died a few weeks ago and, although our courts here in Colorado try to move estate proceedings along at a respectable pace, the judge assigned to Maria's probate proceeding has not yet made a formal personal representative appointment. In all likelihood, however, Phillip will be appointed as personal representative."

"And who will be representing him as his lawyer?"

"That will be up to him."

"Let's get out of the legal weeds here about when beneficiaries of a trust can count on a lawyer representing the trust or the trustee to look out for their interests. I believe you had fiduciary duties to the beneficiaries while you were representing Maria and you breached those duties by not insisting that they be informed of the reduction in their distribution, but those are issues for Judge Elefson to sort out. Did Maria tell you why she decided to reduce what Duane and William would receive at her death?"

"Yes. She said that, during Andy's last few years of life, Duane was mean to him and bullied him. She said

Duane manipulated Billie and she believed Duane was using Billie to front for his illicit drug trafficking activities. She said Duane was belligerent to her and to Phillip. She said Andy would never have wanted his hard-earned wealth to support behavior of the kind Duane had demonstrated. Maria said that, if Andy was still alive, after her death, he would have wanted his wealth to go into the Thurston Family Foundation, to be used in support of pharmaceutical research intended to improve the lives of people all over the world and not the selfish, hedonistic, and possibly criminal pursuits of a child. Those are the reasons Maria gave me for her decision to amend the trust instrument to reduce what Duane and Billie would receive at her death."

"Back to Maria's decision to amend the trust, how old was she when she made that decision?"

"Let's see, she would have been, I believe, seventy-two years old."

"What was her physical and mental condition at that time?"

"By then, she had been diagnosed with a cancer that was likely to take her down. If she was suffering from any kind of dementia or other mental condition, it had not been diagnosed and was not apparent to me. She had an occasional lapse of short-term memory as, I might add, so do I, but I didn't notice any other mental impairment. She absolutely knew what she was doing when she made the decision, as successor trustee of the Thurston Family Trust, to amend the trust instrument and reduce the distributions that would go to Duane and Billie at her death."

"But you were in regular communication with her before she made the decision to give Duane and William a haircut, right?"

"I would say that's correct. I was around and available to her and, if she called, I responded."

"Is your firm now working on the creation of the Thurston Family Foundation?"

"Yes."

"And that's a substantial legal undertaking, is it not? Generating income for your firm?"

"Creating a charitable foundation is a substantial legal undertaking. Charitable foundations function under a complex set of rules set out in the Internal Revenue Code."

"And am I correct that Maria, in amending the trust instrument for the Thurston Family Trust, put you in the position of administering how the money going to Phillip would be distributed and what he could do with that money?"

"Yes."

"And that work would generate fees for your firm, correct?"

"It could, yes."

"And your personal income is affected by work you bring to the firm, correct?

"That's a complicated matter but, basically, yes."

"So what was your personal income last year?"

Me: "Mr. Manifort, I object to that question and am instructing Scott not to answer it. His income is none of your or your clients' business and is not relevant to the issues in this case."

"Well let me make my record, Mr. McConnell. Mr. Freeman's income is totally relevant to this case. He was manipulating his client, Maria, in her capacity as trustee of the Thurston Family Trust, in pursuit of income opportunities for his firm and himself and, in the process, ignoring duties he owed to my clients. That's what my clients' claims against him are all about."

Me: "My objection and instruction to the witness not to answer stands. You'll have to get an order from Judge Elefson requiring an answer if you want to further pursue this matter."

Manifort: "I'll do just that as soon as I get back to Austin. No other questions. Your witness."

Me: "Scott, let's get to the heart of the matter here and not waste any more time. Did you ever advise Maria to reduce the distributions that Duane and Billie would get out of the Thurston Family Trust at her death?"

"No. She made that decision on her own. My only involvement was to tell her, as her lawyer and in my opinion, that she, as the successor trustee of the trust, had the authority to change how the trust's assets would be distributed at her death. And then, once she made her decision, I drafted the amendment to the trust agreement to carry out her decision. But I took no action intended to steer her decision."

"And did you ever have an attorney-client relationship with Duane or Billie?"

"No I did not."

"Did you ever owe them legal duties because they were beneficiaries of the Thurston Family Trust?"

"In my opinion, no. While Maria was alive, my legal duties ran to her, individually and as the trustee of the trust, not to the beneficiaries of the trust."

Manifort decided he had to make a record on that issue, so he made a little speech about lawyers who represent trustees having various duties running to trust beneficiaries and that Scott's opinion on this subject was wrong.

However, he referenced no legal authority to support his position.

After I finished my questions, Manifort was allowed to cover a few more items. He asked about the documents he had received from Scott -- notably his time records and billing statements for work he had done for Andy and Maria -- and after that he shut down the deposition, telling us he had a plane to catch back to Texas. I offered to shake hands. He declined, packed up his briefcase with a noisy flourish and headed out the door. The court reporter asked me a few questions about the spelling of names that had come up during the deposition and then she and the videographer also packed up and left, leaving Scott and me alone.

"So McConnell, how did I do?" (Witnesses always ask this of their lawyer at the end of a deposition, fishing for compliments.)

"You were great, Scott. Much to my surprise, you followed my instructions perfectly. You answered the questions Manifort asked truthfully and precisely, without volunteering additional information. You, of course, will have a chance to review the transcript and make any changes you think are called for. But, assuming there aren't any transcription errors, I don't think you'll want to change anything."

"Good. Time for a drink?"

"Thanks Scott, but no. Veronica is on her way down from Denver and Elsie is due for a potty break."

"So what happens next?"

"We have several options. But we'll talk about that next week. By the way, before I forget, has your malpractice insurer fallen in line and agreed that I can be your lawyer?"

"Yes, no issue there. However, as expected, the insurance company has issued a reservation of rights letter saying it's not on the hook for damages resulting from any intentional wrongful acts on my part, which would include fraud and undue influence."

"And what about the ethics grievance Duane filed with the Supreme Court?"

"The Office of Attorney Regulation Counsel, after she sent me a copy of the grievance, told me I have thirty days to file a response. I assume, as my lawyer, you'll take charge of that."

"Yes, of course, although you'll need to do a first draft to set forth the facts. You need to send me a copy of the grievance but what, basically, does it say?"

"It says that I, as the lawyer for the Thurston Family Trust, owed ethical duties to the trust's beneficiaries -- Duane and Billie -- and I somehow breached those duties by manipulating Maria into amending the trust agreement to the detriment of Duane and Billie without contacting them to tell them what Maria was up to and giving them a chance to challenge her actions."

"Well, we're going to have to hit that nail on the head in any event in the lawsuit Duane has filed, so this will be a good dress rehearsal. For what it's worth, a decision that a rule of professional conduct has been violated does not automatically equate to a basis for liability in a civil lawsuit. And, action that might give rise to liability in a civil lawsuit does not automatically equate to a violation of a rule of professional conduct."

"Well, that's comforting, but I assume you continue to be of the belief that I did nothing wrong and owed no professional duties to Duane and Billie."

"Correct, but this does deserve some further legal scholarship. You might just turn some of your overpaid and really smart associate lawyers at Jensen & Kirkpatrick loose to research the issue and provide us with precedent, if any exists, that you, by acting as Maria's lawyer in connection with her position as trustee of the Thurston Family Trust, didn't also owe duties to the trust's beneficiaries."

"Right. I'll ask one of our associates to research that question. Remind me again, however, never to stick my foot into a trust situation fraught with family acrimony."

"Sure, Scott, I'll remind you again of that, but I did that after the Cranston trust litigation and you blew me off."

"I didn't blow you off. I honored the teary-eyed, pleading request of an old friend and client who was dying. Isn't that what good lawyers are supposed to do?"

"You win. But you still need to promise me you'll be careful the next time the quicksand opens up at your feet."

"Fine. I'll talk to you next week."

Chapter 12

When I got home, Veronica and Elsie were on the porch, enjoying late afternoon warmth before the sun set behind Pikes Peak and the temperature instantly promptly dropped twenty degrees. Veronica was sipping a glass of pinot noir. Elsie had a rawhide bone. After a nice hug and kiss from Veronica, and a respectful tail wag from Elsie, I went inside, poured myself a glass of the pinot noir and joined them.

"So what's going on at the Fed that I should be worrying about? Cyberattacks? Interest rate adjustments? Political intrigue?"

"All of the above," was Veronica's reply. "But, as you know, I'm not allowed to talk to you about any of that."

"Not even political intrigue?"

"No, but if you read the New York Times or the Washington Post, which you do, you'll know everything I know."

"Fair enough. I don't think I want to know more than I already know in any event, unless it's going to cause you to have to go away to some dangerous foreign land for a long period of time. Then I'd be really unhappy."

"No travel plans at the moment. We have enough cyberattacks going on right here at home to keep me busy for months to come. But, not to change the subject or anything, what's going on with Scott, and with R.J.?"

"Scott had his deposition taken today and, although he was worried about it, he performed admirably. The lawsuit against him is probably going to come down to a

technical legal question -- whether or not he owed some kind
of duties to Duane and Billie as trust beneficiaries while he
was representing Maria as trustee of the Thurston Family
Trust. We don't think he did, but our Texas judge is going
to have to rule on that and, as best I can tell, technical
analysis of complex legal issues is not his strong suit. He
was formerly an ambulance chasing personal injury lawyer
before he became a trial court judge, thanks to connections
he had in the Republican party."

"So how is Scott holding up?"

"I worry about that. His blood pressure was not
what you'd want it to be before he got sued, and being
named as a defendant in a lawsuit, and the subject of an
ethical grievance, hasn't helped any. Behind his back, I'm in
regular touch with his wife, Stella, and she and I, and Scott's
and my doctor, Rollie Dumbarton, are watching the situation
as best we can. Scott, as I think you know, despite his
seemingly quiet demeanor, is a strong willed, highly
competitive individual and he has no intention of being
pushed around on the legal stage by the likes of Duane
Thurston. But, in any event, he is indeed showing signs of
stress. I wish I could make it all go away but the legal
system won't allow that to happen, at least not for a while."

"And what about RJ?"

"He's back from Arizona, but he's in a bad way.
He's practically crippled by arthritis and his vision and
hearing are shot. Plus, his much-loved old Winnebago is
falling apart, he has no money to fix it or replace it, and
Abbey, his loyal companion for a dozen years, is also in bad
shape and not likely to make it through the year. His house
is in need of expensive repairs and he has no money for that.
He's not about to agree to move into some kind of assisted

living facility and let me sell his home to pay for that, so I don't know what to do with him, other than let him make his own decisions until he drops. He may be a candidate for a reverse mortgage. I don't like those things but it may be the only way he can stay in his home. Selfishly, I suppose, I've tried to shift this burden onto his kids in Denver, but they haven't risen to the occasion quite to the extent I would like them to."

With that cheery conversation at an end, Veronica and I gave Elsie her dinner and headed out to our own dinner at Le Bistro Saint Tropez, a five-table restaurant in a part of town known as Old Colorado City. Le Bistro Saint Tropez is owned and operated by Georgette DuBois, a short, feisty, well preserved, now mid-seventies lady who was born and raised in Paris and who arrived in this country as the wife of an Air Force pilot. When he was sent off to Vietnam and never came back, she started the restaurant as a way to support herself. The cuisine is south-of-France country, with a touch of Santa Fe thrown in. The prices are fair, and Georgette has a nice selection of affordable wines from parts of France only the locals over there know about. Because, she said, she could never get good help, Georgette does it all -- buying the food, washing the dishes, waiting the tables, cooking the food, cooking the books, etc.

In the beginning, Le Bistro Saint Tropez was open six days a week, lunch and dinner. But it was now down to dinner only, Fridays and Saturdays. And Georgette was sold out to regular customers every night she was open. I slipped us in on late notice this evening only because of a cancellation, and because Georgette likes me, in part because I try to speak French when I'm in the restaurant and she enjoys correcting me.

"Ah, bonjour Jacques. Bonjour Veronique, " she greeted us as we came in the door. Georgette gave us a big smile and a warm "bien venue" and showed us to our table, back in the northwest corner as I had asked. I still remember the first time I took Veronica to Le Bistro Saint Tropez and she, fresh from the East Coast, said something like: "This is nice, not what I expected to find out here in the Wild West." To which I replied: "We have an occasional touch of culture in these parts. Rodeo season lasts only two weeks a year." In any event, we'd been coming to Le Bistro Saint Tropez every chance we could for several years now.

As had become our custom, we ordered a bottle of white wine that came from the town of Auxerre -- just outside the Chablis region of Burgundy. "Just as good, half the price," Georgette had told me many years ago when I first asked how wines from Auxerre compared to the wines that get to carry the valuable Chablis name.

At Le Bistro Saint Tropez, there was no menu. Georgette simply told customers what their three entrée choices were. Tonight, Veronica decided on her favorite, a shrimp dish served with rice and a mix of sautéed vegetables. I ordered the beef stew, which came in a pastry shell – a kind of a glorified potpie, but much better than anything the grocery store had to offer. Slices of a nearly-as-good-as-the-old-country French baguette came first, with a cup of soupe à l'oignon. Dessert, in the French tradition, was a plate of various cheeses, served with delicate little sweet crackers.

Over dinner (and part of a second bottle of wine), I gave Veronica further information about Scott's case, and where I saw it heading. Veronica in turn told me a bit more about the cyber threats facing the United States. As usual, I worked hard to pretend these threats didn't exist or, if they did, that they wouldn't make their way to sleepy Colorado Springs, even though Colorado Springs was home to several military units involved in space and cyber warfare, and could very well be ground zero for an enemy attack. We then headed home to let Elsie out for a final pee and, for me, a nice tuck in from Veronica, followed by the resident neighborhood owl hooting us to sleep.

The next morning, I had Veronica up and moving at an early hour because this was the day, after several years of promising, I was going to further instruct her on the sport of fly fishing. Our destination was Mason Reservoir, a beautiful body of water along the south slope of Pikes Peak owned by the City of Colorado Springs and holding water that is part of the city's precious, never have enough, water supply. For many years -- decades really -- only VIP employees and guests of the city's utilities department were allowed to come here to fish. But, going back maybe five years now, the city had opened the reservoir, four days a week, to licensed Colorado fishermen under strict rules limiting the number of fishermen allowed on any given day, prohibiting wading, and limiting the number of fish that could be harvested. The reservoir is home to a population of brightly colored Colorado cutthroat trout averaging maybe 14 inches in size but going up to 20 inches. These fish are gullible and willingly come to the surface to suck in large (as in big enough to see) dry flies, making this a perfect place to show someone what fly fishing is all about.

The trip to the reservoir involved a one hour drive up into the mountains west of Colorado Springs in the direction of the famous old gold mining towns of Cripple Creek and Victor, and a jog back to the east for a few miles along a gravel road, called Gold Camp Road. It was a nice cloudless morning and, as the sun came up, we had a great view of the Mosquito Range mountains to the west and the Sangre de Cristo mountains to the south.

Once into the fenced and gated reservoir area, and a check-in with the ranger who looks after the property, we had a one-mile uphill hike to the lake, offering a view of a large meadow where moose have been known to hang out. Veronica did OK on this trip, although there were occasional complaints about the absence of a Starbucks, concerns about being out in public before adequate time for makeup, and a noticeable reduction in oxygen at the reservoir's elevation. I explained to Veronica that other fishermen were unlikely to notice makeup issues and she shouldn't worry. However, she was relying on one of my larger baseball hats to minimize the risk. As for the elevation, she adapted quickly to the transition from Colorado Springs at 6,200 feet to the reservoir at 10,900 feet.

The spot I had chosen for Veronica's fly fishing lesson was along the west bank of the reservoir and not far up-lake from the dam. It was bordered by healthy stands of lodgepole and ponderosa pine and granite outcroppings, and provided an unobstructed view of the south summit of Pikes Peak. You could even see the train carrying tourists to the summit.

When we reached our destination, I again tried to explain to Veronica that the idea behind fly fishing was to present to the fish a man-made imitation of a natural insect and that the delivery mechanism for this artificial insect came from the fly line. In other words, the fishman would try to deliver the fly to the fish by throwing the line out onto the water, with the artificial fly attached to the end of the fly line using something called a tippet -- a length of transparent monofilament material intended to help the fly look natural to the fish. The fly rod is designed to enhance throwing the fly line out into the water to the location you're trying to reach, and with a gentle landing of the fly at the targeted location. It sounds easy, but practice is needed to be competent.

After this introductory lecture, I handed to Veronica a fly rod I had already prepared for her use, with a fly line in place held by a reel. I had attached to the end of the fly line a seven-foot leader with a three foot tippet and, at the end of the tippet, a big fuzzy imitation of some kind of insect Mother Nature would not recognize but that a trout might consider a meal.

On her first attempt at casting the fly line into the water, Veronica snagged the branch of a ponderosa pine behind her. After that issue was resolved, she tried again and managed to get the fly line, and the attached tippet and fly, out into the water a distance of maybe 30 feet from the shore. This was not an ideal distance but, in furtherance of the premise that cutthroat trout like to cruise along the bank of whatever body of water they are in, I told Veronica she had done well for a first of the day cast and to leave the fly alone. I then went to work setting up a second rod, line, leader, tippet and fly for my use.

I was halfway through that effort when Veronica let out a scream.

"Jack, oh my God, I've caught a fish. I saw it come up from underneath and grab the fly. Oh my God. Now what do I do?"

"Just let the fish take out line. Don't try to jerk it back toward you. You need to tire the fish out a bit before we bring it to net. Otherwise, you could break your line or hurt the fish. Once you feel the pressure on the line diminish a bit, start to reel in the line. But, when the fish takes off again, let it go."

"Oh my God, it's still tugging. And my hands are shaking. And I need a glass of wine or a cigarette or something."

"Veronica, you're doing great. Just keep tension on the line but let the fish take line when it wants to. Keep the tip of your rod up a bit. This allows the rod to act like a shock absorber and helps to tire the fish without breaking the line."

Although by now Veronica's entire body was shaking and she was muttering to herself using words I didn't know she knew, and that her mother would never approve of, she eventually tired the fish and was able to bring it close enough to shore for me to scoop it up in a landing net. I quickly removed the barbless hook from the fish, which was maybe 16 inches in length and beautifully colored with blues and greens and yellows and multi-colored spots. I let Veronica hold the fish in her hands for a brief moment while I took a photo of this historic event. I then put the fish back in the water, stroking its back until it was breathing regularly, and let it swim away, assuming it had learned something useful about what it decides to eat.

We spent a total of three hours at the lake and Veronica caught another five fish. She calmed down after the first fish and her casting improved with each try. She was now able to get the fly farther out from shore, closer to where the fish usually hang out. Only once did she again catch a branch of one of the trees behind her. I also hooked up with half a dozen of these obliging fish, all on big-enough-to-see flies. All fish were returned to the lake unharmed.

On the trip back to Colorado Springs, Veronica engaged in non-stop gushing about her experience and authorized me to buy for her a rod, reel, line, waders, wading shoes, flies, tippet material, fishing vest, strike indicators, instructional videos, Orvis-approved fishing fashions, and whatever else I thought she might need to leap into fly fishing fully equipped. I tried to explain to her that I already had extras of many of these items, but I'm not sure she was listening. And I was thinking to myself, I've created a monster. My calming, pleasant, all by myself, stress reducing days of fly fishing were probably over.

After a Starbucks stop in Woodland Park, we motored on to Colorado Springs and found Elsie sprawled out on the sofa, showing no sign that she missed us while we were away. We had an early dinner of warmed-over pizza, watched a few innings of the Rockies losing effort against the Los Angeles Dodgers and went to bed early. Veronica was out like a light. No snuggle on the menu. Elsie and I were close behind.

Chapter 13

The next morning, Sunday, Veronica hung out with Elsie and me until 10:30 but then, after a long kiss and hug, she was off to Denver to get a head start on the week to come, which included a visit by the chairman of the Federal Reserve Board to the Federal Reserve Bank in Denver. Veronica was a part of the team put in place to be sure this event went smoothly, and did not result in any kind of political damage or embarrassment.

After Veronica left, and Elsie and I had put in a lengthy walk up into the foothills to the west of my neighborhood, I checked my office emails. I found there an email from Scott, sent late yesterday, telling me to call him as soon as possible.

"Hi Scott. What's up?"

"Jack, we have another problem. As I think you know, my son Jeff is a math teacher at a high school west of Denver. For several years, he has also coached his school's girls volleyball team. He was an all-American volleyball player at the University of Colorado and the teams he has coached have been very successful, regionally and even nationally. Well, somebody has anonymously posted on some social media website called InstaFlip a claim that Jeff has been engaging in inappropriate touching, and making sexually suggestive statements, involving members of the girls volleyball team. And this posting has, at the speed of light, made it to the parents of kids who are now, and have been in the past, members of the team, as well as members of the school's administration. And the information in the post is showing up in internet searches. A small, but hysterical, group of these parents have gone to the superintendent of schools and members of the school board and demanded an investigation, and that Jeff be fired, both as a teacher and as a coach, and prosecuted for sexual abuse of a minor by a person in a position of trust. Since school boards and school administrators always fall off the log on the side of unhappy parents, Jeff has now been put on administrative leave, fortunately with pay, and the school district has taken possession of his laptop and his cell phone. He and his wife are pretty upset, as you might expect, and so am I. This is an intentional act of reputation injury but it's likely going to be difficult to find the source of the post since it's been routed through multiple cloud servers involving encryption. It's amazing how simple it is to anonymously destroy someone's reputation on the internet. I think, but have absolutely no evidence, that Duane Thurston could be behind this."

"Wow. I didn't think Duane would let his anger and his greed put him that far out of bounds. I hope he doesn't own guns, although that's probably wishful thinking. But here's what I suggest as a strategy. The Colorado Educators Association, a union to which Jeff is undoubtedly a member, employs lawyers to represent teachers who get caught up in a disciplinary issue like this. I know a couple of these lawyers and they are very good. I'll call one of them in the morning and ask him to jump on this on behalf of Jeff. I'll also turn Veronica loose to see what she can drum up about the source of this posting. And I think it's time to bring in Ed, the private investigator who helped us with the Cranston litigation. Fighting fire with fire is not how lawyers are trained to resolve disputes, but it seems to me we have no choice here. If Duane is really behind this, it would seem to be time to take him on at a different level."

"OK, I guess. I have no other thoughts other than -- should I resign as the successor trustee of the Thurston Family Trust?"

"No. Maybe down the road a bit, but not yet. You made a moral commitment to Maria to carry out her instructions with regard to the trust. As you know better than me, the law of trusts would allow you to bail and ask a court to appoint another trustee. But I know you well enough to know that you would never feel right about walking away from a commitment you made to a client, and a friend. Plus, your resigning as trustee won't end the lawsuit Duane has brought against you. He claims you manipulated Maria -- asserted undue influence over her -- for your own selfish benefit and your resigning as trustee would get played out in court as an admission of liability on your part. So, you need to stay in the saddle, whether you want to or not."

"I get it. Remind me again, when the time comes, not to agree to be anybody's trustee."

"Scott, as I hope I've told you, people sometimes need a lawyer who has the balls, or female equivalent, to take on a difficult situation, so don't bail quite yet on all such opportunities. You just need to be a little more selective."

On Monday, I called one of the lawyers I know at the Colorado Educators Association, Charlie Justin, and asked if he could take charge of representing Jeff Freeman in connection with the school district's actions in response to the reputation assassination that was now underway. Charlie is a big Black guy who played professional football -- a

linebacker -- before going to law school at the University of
Colorado. He is smart, tough, and knows his way around in
the highly political world of school boards. He and I worked
together several years ago when a teacher here in Colorado
Springs had been falsely accused of theft of school property
and found herself dealing with the guilty-until-proven-
innocent way school districts seem to behave. Charlie was
able to track down the real thief and we were able to have
the teacher reinstated with full pay, a damages award, an
untarnished employment record, and a public apology.

"Hi Jack. Good to talk to you. I'll try to get myself
assigned to that matter. No promises, but the powers that be
around here usually listen to me on case assignments. These
cases are tough, of course, because the parents go crazy and
school board members, as aspiring politicians who think
they'll be president someday, are hell bent on appeasing the
parents. In this swamp, right and wrong, and verifiable
facts, don't seem to matter much."

I then, with Scott's permission, told Charlie a few
things about Duane Thurston's campaign to change the
distribution of the assets of the Thurston Family Trust by
going after Jeff's father and claiming he had engaged in
undue influence with Maria. Since we had no proof that
Duane was behind the character assassination of Jeff
Freeman as a way to get at Scott, Charlie and I agreed we
would not make any claim along those lines but we would
keep an eye on that ball.

I next put in a call to Ed, the private investigator
Scott and I had worked with in another complicated trust
matter involving a missing will. Ed's real name is Winfred
Siegel Wyzowski, III, but not many people know that. I
know it because the first time I used him, I wanted to be sure

he in fact had a private investigator's license, which he does -- from Louisiana, where the requirements for a background check are minimal. But he's generally known in the trade just as Ed and his training and experience are not things you discuss with him.

Ed helped me on a complicated bank embezzlement case maybe fifteen years ago and was recommended to me -- informally and off the record -- by the Federal Deposit Insurance Corporation. He did very good work and uncovered a clever and well-hidden conspiracy among tellers to steal cash out of teller drawers at branches of the bank involved located in four different states.

Then, I hired him a few years later in a case against a stock brokerage firm. That firm had a client it let give investment advice to other clients, generating business for the firm. This guy was using insider information about the quantity of frozen hog carcasses in packing plant warehouses in Iowa to recommend investments in pork belly futures. It turned out he was an ex-con, convicted of stealing frozen meat from these same warehouses. He still had buddies in the warehouses and they were giving him the confidential information he was using to advise the brokerage firm's clients. He had a great track record until his sources dried up, and then the brokerage firm's clients lost a ton of money. They demanded an investigation but the brokerage firm stonewalled them, so we had to sue. Thanks to Ed's investigative work, the investors recovered all their losses and received a small amount of punitive damages. And the brokerage firm was put on a short probationary leash by its regulatory agency, FINRA -- the Financial Industry Regulatory Authority

My most recent work with Ed involved a cashier's check fraud and a money laundering operation. He again did a great job, tracking down the criminals and sending them to prison, and recovering the money they had stolen and were trying to hide in offshore accounts.

Ed lives in a motor home and prefers not to be in one spot for very long, but I had his very private and encrypted cell phone number and he always returns my calls. Ed charges $200 an hour for routine hours. He charges $600 an hour for what he calls "home run" hours. You have to trust him on this but you'll know a home run hour when he has one.

"Well hello Jack. Good to hear from you. I'm in my motor home on the way to Las Vegas to participate in a televised poker tournament. You may remember I've done that a few times in the past and apparently I now have a loyal television following, although I always wear a disguise and use a made-up name. In any event, they've invited me back. I never win much money at these events but the hotel sponsoring the tournament gives me the money to gamble with and puts me up for a few days in a nice suite, and feeds me. So what's up that I can help you with?"

I then gave Ed a brief rundown on Duane Thurston's claims against Scott and his possible illicit drug activity, and our suspicion that he might be behind the defamation of Scott's son, Jeff.

"I think we're looking for evidence that Duane Thurston is in fact illegally dealing in addictive prescription pain medicines and that he may have orchestrated the reputation attack on Scott's son, Jeff Freeman. I'm not sure what we'll do with any information you come up with but we can't let Duane run amuck. My first priority in all of this is to get Scott out of under the stress Duane Thurston is causing him."

"Got it. Send me all the info you think I should have about Duane Thurston and the Thurston Family Trust, and a link to the social media post that has targeted Jeff. You can use my encrypted email account, as usual. I'll scratch around a bit on this while I'm in Las Vegas and get back to you."

"Thanks Ed. Good luck with the poker tournament. I'll watch for you on TV."

Chapter 14

The following Wednesday, it was time for me to take Duane Thurston's deposition. Since he was living in Texas and not Colorado, and the lawsuit he filed against Scott was docketed in Texas, I had no way to force him to come to Colorado for the deposition. So, he was in Austin and the deposition was being conducted remotely, using a Zoom connection. Duane and Manafort, and a court reporter I had hired, were in a conference room at Manafort's offices. I was in one of the small conference rooms (the one decorated with fishing paraphernalia...) at my office. Zoom would let me create a video of the deposition. Hence, there was no need to hire a videographer.

This was my first occasion to get a look at Duane Thurston. I couldn't see much on the virtual connection but he appeared to be short – maybe five foot six inches – in reasonably good shape, with no facial hair, and a receding hair line. He was, I knew from Scott, forty-eight years old. He was wearing a Dallas Cowboys tee shirt and shorts, showing no respect for the legal process associated with a lawsuit. His facial expression was somewhere between irritated to have to be there and pretend boredom.

Manafort began the deposition with a short on the record speech stating that the deposition was improper under some Texas rule of procedure I have never heard of and which made no sense to me, and should therefore not be available for use at a trial. I responded that I disagreed, referencing no legal authority -- because I had none -- and we then continued.

"Mr. Thurston, as you know, I represent Scott
Freeman, the lawyer you and your brother William – we call
him Billie -- have sued in this lawsuit. Let me start by
asking you to tell me your current employment."

Manafort, as he would continue to do for the next
hour, objected to this question, and every other question I
asked, as irrelevant. But, he instructed his client to go ahead
and answer.

"Sure. I manage a taxicab company that operates
here in Austin and in Colorado Springs."

"And how did you become involved in that line of
work?"

"Friend of a friend."

"Did you ever work in the pharmaceutical industry?"

"I worked a couple of years for my father's
company, PharmOne."

"What did you do in that job?"

"I purchased inventory for the company's retail
stores."

"Including pain medicines, such as oxycontin?"

"Sure. Those medicines were stocked in our stores."

"Have you been acquiring and selling those drugs
outside the normal pharmaceutical distribution system, on
the street?"

"OBJECTION," Manafort shouted. "Duane, don't
answer that question?"

"And the basis for your objection?" I asked.

"Relevance, and intent to harass the witness."

"Do you know Jeff Freeman?"

"No. Never heard of him."

"He is Scott's son, a high school math teacher in
Colorado."

"What's that got to do with anything?"

"Someone posted a false accusation about him on a social media website, and it caused him to be suspended from his teaching position. We've been concerned it might have been you."

"That's ridiculous. What evidence do you have to support that outrageous statement?"

Manafort: "That's enough McConnell. Let's get on to something relevant to this lawsuit."

Me: "Well, to make a record here, we think Mr. Thurston filed this lawsuit to harass Scott Freeman as Maria Thurston's lawyer, as the successor trustee to the Thurston Family Trust, and as an incorporator of the Thurston Family Foundation, and we think he may be defaming Scott's son as part of his campaign of harassment, all of which is aimed at extorting an additional amount for himself and Billie out of the Thurston Family Trust. That's the basis of Scott Freeman's counterclaim in this case and my questions are all very relevant to the counterclaim. And we think the ethics complaint he filed against Scott Freeman with the Colorado Supreme Court falls into the same bucket."

My purpose here was to give Duane something to worry about and, if Ed or Veronica found evidence linking Duane to the Jeff Freeman defamation, his denial in this deposition would play out as an under oath lie -- perjury. Same thing with his denial of illicit drug activity.

"Mr. Thurston, tell me about your relationship with your stepmother, Maria."

"She went out of her way to sabotage my and Billie's relationship with our father."

"In what way?"

"She made sure it was hard for us to see Andy, and she fed him all kinds of made-up bullshit about our behavior. She didn't like us and tried to do everything in her power to cause Andy not to like us. This was all a scheme on her part to be sure Andy's wealth went mostly to Phillip and not to Billie and me. Andy didn't buy into that strategy, but once he was dead, Maria felt she was free to carry out the strategy on her own, and that's what she did."

"So what evidence do you have that Scott Freeman was unduly influencing Maria?"

"He was constantly pushing her in the direction of screwing Billie and me, and favoring Phillip. He totally abused his position as her lawyer to manipulate her decision making. She didn't come up with the idea of amending the trust agreement for the Thurston Family Trust by herself. That came from Freeman, and he set himself up nicely to have all kinds of lucrative legal work creating and running the Thurston Family Foundation, managing Phillip's affairs because he was allegedly unable to manage his own money, administering Maria's estate, and conducting the on-going business of the Thurston Family Trust. He did all of that and hung Billie and me out to dry in the process."

"Mr. Thurston, I'm looking for facts, not your opinion. Can you point to anything specific that Scott Freeman did to manipulate Maria's decision making?"

"He told her she could amend the trust."

"Don't you think that was a legal opinion given in response to a question from a client?"

"No. He was feeding her a bullshit opinion of questionable validity with the intent and expectation that she would amend the trust agreement, to his personal benefit."

"Anything else you can point to as an act of undue influence?"

"Not right now but I'm sure there is other stuff he did. I'll think about it and get back to you, through my lawyer."

"Are you married?"

"No."

"Have you ever been married?"

"No."

"Have you ever been charged with domestic violence?"

Manifort: "OBJECTION. Relevance. Intent to intimidate the witness. Duane, don't answer that question. Mr. McConnell, what the hell does this have to do with anything remotely related to this lawsuit?"

Me: "Oh come on Carlton, it's our position in this case, as you well know, that Maria changed the trust agreement because she thought your client was a bad person and her late husband, Andy, would not have wanted him to receive a big chunk of the wealth he had created with PharmOne. So, an arrest for domestic violence fits nicely into the mold of a bad person, and when we try this case, Duane's past behavior is going to be center stage."

Me again: "Just a few more questions, Mr. Thurston."

"No. I've had enough of this crap. I'm leaving."

At which point, Duane got up and stormed out of the room, knocking over the court reporter's stenographic machine on the way.

Me, once the court reporter was back in business: "Well, I don't consider this deposition concluded, so we'll treat this as an adjournment, at the witness's request. And, we'll continue it at a later date."

Manifort: "I believe the deposition is at an end. Mr. McConnell has had his shot at the witness and he is not entitled to reconvene the proceedings, especially since his intent is intimidation."

Me: "Whatever. We're done for the day." And we then disconnected from Zoom.

After the deposition, I called Scott to report on the events of the day.

"So how did it go?" he wanted to know.

"No surprises. He had no facts to support his allegations of undue influence other than your close contact with Maria as her lawyer and you telling her that, in your opinion, she could amend the trust agreement if that's what she wanted to do. He denied having any knowledge of, or any role in, the defamation of your son. Manifort wouldn't let him answer questions about illicit drug sales or domestic violence arrests. He made a well-rehearsed speech about Maria trying to impede his and Billie's relationship with their father, and her intent to make sure Phillip, and not Duane and Billie, got the bulk of the funds being distributed out of the trust. And then he walked out."

"Jack, Jeff's situation is rapidly deteriorating. His wife is modestly hysterical, with her friends shunning her for being married to a sexual predator. And his children are being shunned by their friends because their parents have told them not to hang out with Jeff Freeman's children. And all but three members of the girls volleyball team have quit, ordered to do so by their parents, so there is no more team."

"All to be expected, I guess. I can report, however, that Charlie Justin has received permission from the

Colorado Educators Association to represent Jeff, and he has a meeting set up with the school district's attorney for Friday. She's a newly minted lawyer named Louisa Gardner who, I've been told, is trying to build a reputation as a scorched earth hard ass. But Charlie is good at dealing with lawyers like that and he will, in a diplomatic kind of way, make sure she and the school district -- and its board of education -- know the district is heading for a big time, expensive, bad publicity legal shoot out if it doesn't back off and put Jeff back in the classroom. So, not to change the subject or anything, but how are you and Stella holding out?"

"I guess we're doing OK. Neither of us is sleeping worth a damn. Stella spends her days fretting about what's happening to Jeff and wanting to help and not knowing how to help. And I'm finding it hard to concentrate at work. I've got clients with some really complex tax issues in the pipeline and I can't seem to focus on their issues. Tax law, unlike what you do for a living, requires your brain to fire on all cylinders. And, I'm now spending too much of my time working on a response to the grievance that Duane filed with the Colorado Supreme Court. I'll have my draft of the response to you in the next couple of days for your review, completion and filing. Isn't there a way to shut all of this down?"

"Sure Scott. You could ignore the wishes of Maria, your client and friend who is now dead, and give Duane and Billie the money Duane wants them to have. But how are you going to feel if you sell your client – and friend -- down the river to protect your own butt? Maria won't care, because she'd dead, but what's on the bubble here is your commitment to a client – and friend -- with whom you can no longer communicate and your conscience. However this ends, you need to be at peace with yourself. So, my advice is -- take deep breaths and hang in there. And take up fishing."

Chapter 15

Since Duane Thurston's deposition didn't take as long as I had expected -- because he elected to walk out -- I had time Wednesday afternoon to pay a visit to RJ. I knocked on the front door of RJ's house and, when he didn't answer, I went inside. I immediately heard the engine of the Winnebago running and smelled exhaust fumes, and headed to the garage.

The garage door and windows were closed and there was a hose running from the tailpipe of the Winnebago into the cab. I pulled open the driver's side door and found RJ slumped over the steering wheel. Abby was in the passenger seat and her head was resting in RJ's lap. Abby was dead. RJ was unconscious but still had a weak pulse.

I hesitated, but then slowly closed the car door, left the motor running, went back into the house, sat down in the kitchen -- and cried. On the kitchen table, RJ had neatly set out his will, a life insurance policy, bank and other account statements, a contacts list, and a list of his computer log-ons. Plus this note, done with his computer and printer:

"Jack, I assume you'll be the first to find me, so thanks for everything you have done to help me and for all the great fishing trips we've had. You knew it had to end this way. Because of my arthritis, my wife's death, and everything else that's been going on these last couple of years, I've had no life left. I have no interest in endless -- and useless -- doctor visits and giving what little

wealth I have left to the health care industry.
As we have often discussed, death is not a
matter of if, it's a matter of when and how.
And, as we always told our clients,
sometimes all you have left to deal with
whatever curve balls life has thrown at you
is a menu of bad choices. So, pick your best
bad choice and run with it. That's what I
have done. Although I struggled with this, I
decided Abby needed to take this journey
with me. She has also been suffering
chronic pain and she has gone blind and
deaf. No more interest in tennis balls or
anything else. She and I have shared life
together and it seemed right that we should
share death together. She told me, in her
own way, this is what she wanted as well.
See if you can get us cremated together. In
all events, please include a tennis ball when
Abby is cremated and please spread our
ashes together, as we have discussed, up at
the west end of Eleven Mile Canyon, next to
the river. I want you to have my fishing
gear, including my new Orvis 4 weight,
which I never had a chance to use. My
waders have a couple of leaks, but you can
probably fix them. Call my kids and tell
them I had a peaceful end, and as I wanted it
to be. Take care.

Your friend, RJ"

I stayed in RJ's kitchen for another twenty minutes, my mind a blank, until the engine to the Winnebago shut off because it was out of gas. I went back in the garage to confirm that RJ was dead and then called the Manitou Springs police to let them know they needed to come to RJ's house to retrieve a dead body, dead by suicide. I picked up Abby's body and took it home with me, not knowing what the police would do with it. I put her body on Elsie's dog bed and Elsie curled up next to it, and stayed there through the night. In the morning, I would take the body to Heidi Freeman, my vet, to see if she could find a way to have RJ and Abby cremated together and, if not, at least be sure Abby was cremated with one of her favorite tennis balls. I called RJ's kids in Denver and told them he was gone, in the way he had wanted. I told them I would see to the administration of his estate and otherwise deal with the legal complexities of death. They needed to do whatever family members do in a circumstance like this, to include sifting through and disposing of his personal property, other than his fishing gear which I would take care of. They wanted to talk, but I was in no mood for that, so my calls to them were brief.

I headed out to my deck with a bottle of pinot noir -- RJ's favorite beverage when he wasn't drinking whiskey -- and watched the sun set behind Pikes Peak. There were no clouds, and Venus hung brightly over the north slope of the mountain for a long time. It was a sleepless night, full of troubling thoughts about what I had done -- or hadn't done.

Chapter 16

Thursday morning, I took Abby's body to Heidi's veterinary clinic. She said it wouldn't be possible to cremate RJ and Abby together -- she'd been down that road before. So I gave her one of Abby's tennis balls -- she had many -- and Heidi assured me it would be included in Abby's cremation. I then headed to my office and told everyone there -- they all knew RJ -- that he was dead, no details, and that we would be handling his estate. I gave his will to Stephanie, with instructions to file it with the probate court as the first step in the estate administration process.

I also called Scott and Veronica and told them we had lost RJ, to suicide. However, I didn't tell them he was still alive when I found him. That information, I decided, needed to remain with me. I obtained modest comfort from the fact that RJ had signed the do not resuscitate instruction I had prepared for him, at his request, a year ago, but I also knew such an instruction legally only came into play when someone's heart stopped. Arguably, then, I had assisted a suicide, which would be a crime of homicide under Colorado law. Colorado has an assisted suicide law, but it contains requirements that clearly hadn't been met in this instance.

I told myself that what I had done was an act of friendship, and RJ would not have wanted me to be charged with a crime for having helped him end his life in the manner he had chosen. RJ would also not have wanted me to lose my law license, although that would be a likely outcome if I was charged with a homicide. I wanted to talk this out with someone who had authority to grant me legal immunity, divine absolution, moral forgiveness. That, however, was not an option, at least not yet. At some point, I might decide to hire a lawyer to whom I could tell, under the protection of the attorney-client privilege, that RJ still had a pulse when I found him. But then lawyers sometimes have a duty to report a crime they learn about from a client, so I wasn't sure hiring a lawyer as a confessor was the right way to go. Maybe there was a priest available to whom I could tell all, protected by the clergy privilege, but I hadn't set foot in a church for a long time and wasn't sure I would be welcome. I really wanted to tell Scott and Veronica what had happened. This, however, could expose them to a claim of obstruction of justice, also a crime. So, I was left to make peace with my own conscience. I did tell the entire story to Elsie who, when I was done, put her head in my lap, wagged her tail gently, and let me know it was OK -- that, even if I had committed a homicide, she still loved me.

Later in the day on Thursday, Ed checked in. He was in Las Vegas, the poker tournament was heading in a positive direction, and he had started to scratch around concerning the internet defamation of Jeff Freeman. He was able to tell me the internet post that led to the accusations against Jeff had come from an anonymous source and had been routed through several encrypted in-the-cloud channels, and had been customized to reach the parents of volleyball team members, the members of the school board and the school district's executive management team, meaning the superintendent of schools and the various department heads. Ed said it looked like we were dealing with someone who knew precisely how to hide behind the identity protection devices offered by the internet. Ed told me, not surprisingly, that he had contacts in the internet security world -- some of whom sought to protect data and some of whom sought to steal it -- and he thought they might be able to help him drill down to the source of the post accusing Jeff of inappropriate behavior involving members of his school's girls volleyball team. Veronica, I knew, also had internet security contacts but, as an employee of the Fed, her hands were tied. Nonetheless, in furtherance of her duties to keep up on internet activities that might be a threat to the United States, she would make a few discrete inquiries and share with Ed anything useful she might learn.

    After another restless night, on Friday I forced myself to deal with the grievance Duane Thurston had filed against Scott with the Office of Attorney Regulation Counsel. This office is an agency of the Colorado Supreme Court and it prosecutes grievances against Colorado lawyers claiming a violation of the Rules of Professional Conduct. Overseeing the work of the Attorney Regulation Counsel is something called the Attorney Regulation Committee, whose nine members are lawyers, judges and (to bring sanity to the process) a couple of people not otherwise involved with the legal profession. Then, there is an official called the Presiding Disciplinary Judge who hears and decides cases that require a trial for resolution.

    Duane obviously had had some help preparing his grievance. It weaved together provisions from the Uniform Trust Code setting out the duties a trustee has to keep trust beneficiaries informed of the administrative activities of a trust with provisions of the Rules of Professional Conduct which require lawyers to treat non-clients honestly. Duane's basic pitch in his grievance was that Scott had violated the Rules of Professional Conduct by not informing two of the trust's beneficiaries -- Duane and Billie -- that Maria was intending to amend the trust agreement to reduce their shares. In effect, Duane had repackaged the lawsuit he filed against Scott in a court in Texas into an ethical violation grievance. Although, as I had told Scott, a finding that a violation of the Rules of Professional Conduct had occurred doesn't equate to a successful civil lawsuit for damages, it makes for good theater in the trial of such a lawsuit. So, if the grievance against Scott results in a finding that he committed an ethical violation, Duane could use that as background noise in the trial of his claim for damages. If the grievance results in a dismissal, that event would have no bearing on the outcome of Duane's lawsuit and most likely Judge Elefson wouldn't even allow the jury to know the grievance had been filed or its dismissal.

This was all very clever on Duane's part. The basic purpose of the grievance was to harass and threaten Scott but if the grievance actually resulted in a finding that Scott had violated the Rules of Professional Conduct, Duane would have created for himself a nice piece of evidence supporting his theory that Scott was a greedy, manipulative lawyer intent on creating legal business for himself. If the grievance went nowhere, Duane's position in his lawsuit against Scott was not impaired. So, might score points; can't lose points. If the grievance was dismissed, I might be able to use the filing of the grievance as evidence in support of Scott's counterclaim for abuse of process, but that would likely be a hard sell to Judge Elefson since grievances are dismissed for lots of reasons, or no reason, and a dismissal wouldn't prove that the grievance was frivolous or that it had been filed with an evil motive.

Scott had done a good job, in the initial draft of a response to the grievance that I'd asked him to prepare, setting out the facts. He had a long relationship with Andy and Maria as their lawyer. After Andy died, his representation of Maria included advising her on her duties as successor trustee of the Thurston Family Trust. At Maria's instruction, he had drafted the amendment to the trust agreement that reduced the amount Duane and Billie would receive at Maria's death. He had told Maria that, in his opinion, she had authority to amend the trust agreement in the manner she was intending. He had not advised her that she, as trustee, might have an obligation to notify the affected trust beneficiaries -- Duane and Billie -- of her intentions and she had never presented that question to him. He had not coached Maria in any way to reduce the distributions coming to Duane and Billie. She had made that decision on her own. As the successor trustee of the Thurston Family Trust after Maria's death, he, Scott, had been administering the trust, and intended to continue to administer the trust, in keeping with the terms of the trust agreement, including the amendment that gave Duane and Billie their haircut.

It was now my turn to work on the legal arguments to be included in the response and I first made sure it was clear that, from Scott's and my point of view, Duane's grievance had been filed as a tactic to gain leverage over Scott in a civil lawsuit pending in Texas wherein Duane and Billie were suing him for the millions of dollars that Maria's amendment to the trust agreement was costing them. I next made the point, well known to the Office of Attorney Regulation Counsel, that facts which might support a claim for damages in a civil lawsuit did not necessarily equate to a violation of the Rules of Professional Conduct and a valid grievance.

Jim Flynn

It was then time to drill down on the provisions in the Rules of Professional Conduct that Duane claimed were violated. Duane's grievance was based in large part on the premise that Scott was a lawyer representing the Thurston Family Trust and therefore the beneficiaries of the trust -- meaning Duane and Billie -- were also his clients. Under the Rules of Professional Conduct, a lawyer has a duty to keep a client "reasonably informed about the status of the matter" the lawyer is working on and Scott, the grievance said, breached that duty when he didn't tell Duane and Billie that Maria was planning to, and did, amend the trust agreement to greatly reduce what they would receive out of the trust when Maria died.

To respond to this claim, I had to delve into the murky waters of trust law and argue that Scott's client was Maria and not the Thurston Family Trust. Trusts aren't a separate legal entity, like a corporation and, legally, they are embodied in the person of the trustee. An individual serving as trustee is entitled to separate legal representation. In other words, the trustee of a trust can hire a lawyer to advise the trustee on issues affecting the trustee's duties and this doesn't cause the lawyer to owe duties to trust beneficiaries. Furthermore, communications between the trustee and the trustee's lawyer are covered by the attorney-client privilege. That means, I argued, that third parties, including trust beneficiaries, have no right to stick their nose under the tent and be privy to communications between the trustee and the trustee's lawyer. In fact, if Scott had informed Duane and Billie of Maria's plans to amend the trust agreement to cut down the amount Duane and Billie would receive at Maria's death, I argued that he would indeed have violated the Rules of Professional Conduct by disclosing a client confidence.

112

I then had to deal with a section of the Colorado
Trust Code which says a trustee must keep beneficiaries
"reasonably informed about the administration of the trust
and of material facts necessary for them to protect their
interest." Maybe this meant Maria should have told Duane
and Billie of her intention to reduce what they would receive
out of the trust when she dies but, I argued, it doesn't impose
a duty on a lawyer representing a trustee to keep
beneficiaries informed of administrative matters affecting
their interests. Nor does it impose a duty on a lawyer
representing a trustee to inform the trustee of her possible
duties along those lines. In all events, I was hopeful that
Attorney Regulation Counsel -- Jocelyn Alvarez -- would
not see fit to ding Scott for not answering questions Maria
never asked about her duties as trustee.

I also had to deal with Duane's argument that, once
Maria died and Scott became trustee and did in fact have
duties to beneficiaries of the trust, he should have advised
Duane and Billie to go to court and challenge Maria's right
to amend the trust agreement to their detriment. But, by the
time Scott took over as successor trustee, Duane knew about
Maria's amendment to the trust agreement and he could have
sought independent legal counsel to challenge the
amendment if he thought what Maria did went beyond her
authority. In any event, in Scott's opinion, Maria's
amendment to the trust agreement was wholly within her
rights as successor trustee, so there was nothing to challenge.

I finalized the response and asked Stephanie to put it
in a proper format and file it (electronically) with the Office
of Attorney Regulation Counsel. We would know soon
enough if the grievance would be dismissed for failure to
present evidence of a grievable offense or force us to move

on to the next level. I emailed the final response to Scott and told him we were now, for better or for worse, at the mercy of the attorney disciplinary system, confusing though it was.

Chapter 17

The following Wednesday, we had a case
management conference with Judge Elefson. Manifort chose
to appear in person, allowing him time alone with the judge.
I appeared via a Zoom connection. This was my first chance
to see Judge Elefson in action. No surprises there. He
looked and acted like a Colorado trial court judge, only with
a Texas accent and a string tie. As is typical in the world of
trial courts, at this stage of the proceedings the judge had no
real understanding what this case was about. So Manifort
and I each gave him our view of that. Manifort said the case
was about undue influence of an elderly woman by a greedy
Colorado lawyer. I told the judge the case was about
Manifort's clients -- Duane and Billie, but really Duane --
trying to extort money out of a successor trustee after the
previous trustee, now dead, had reduced their distributions.
No response from the judge as to any of that. He merely
conducted his usual judicial business by establishing
deadlines for discovery, limiting expert witnesses to one for
each side, and setting a trial date. We were now on his
docket for a four-day jury trial, two months down the road,
in mid-July.

We were on a trailing docket, meaning two other
cases had priority over ours. If those cases didn't settle, we
would be bumped off the trial calendar and required to
reschedule. This is how courts run the show these days
since many cases settle and court administrators (and
taxpayers) don't want judges sitting around with nothing to
do. However, the cases having priority over ours were both
auto accident personal injury cases and these cases almost

always settle. That's because the lawyers representing the plaintiffs have a contingent fee arrangement in place and, in my experience, at least, they don't want to risk taking a case to trial where they might actually have to do a great deal of work and, if they lose, get nothing for their effort. So, they convince their clients to settle for less than what their case might really be worth and before the lawyer has to do much work.

Judge Elefson also ordered us to engage in mediation, standard practice these days for trial court judges dealing with what they, at least, think are crowded dockets. Mediation can result in settlements, thereby reducing those dockets.

After we were done with the judge, Manifort and I got on the phone and talked about how we would handle mediation. We agreed this could be done virtually, with a Zoom setup. He said he would come up with a list of mediators in the Austin area and I said I would look at his list and see if any of them were acceptable to Scott and me. Since experienced mediators don't let themselves get a reputation that they favor any particular lawyer, I was confident I could find someone acceptable on Manifort's list. I was also confident mediation wasn't going to generate a settlement in this case. Even though I might encourage Scott to do so, I felt he would never agree to sell Maria's last wishes down the river with a settlement that gave additional money to Duane and Billie in order to settle a claim that had been brought against him personally.

After the status conference and the follow-up call with Manifort concerning mediation, I checked in with Scott by phone and told him of the day's events. He sounded tired, thanked me for my efforts on his behalf, said the administration of Maria's estate was moving along, and told me other lawyers at his firm were busy working on establishing the Thurston Family Foundation in accordance with the terms set out in the trust instrument for the Thurston Family Trust.

I then headed home to sit on the porch for a few minutes with Elsie. She had a stuffed dragon with her for comfort. I had a chardonnay. I explained to Elsie what was going on with my friend Scott and how he was being made to pay a steep price for being a good lawyer. Elsie seemed to understand and expressed sympathy.

It was a nice Colorado spring evening. Springtime in the Rockies is a mix of powder blue skies with pleasant temperatures, bitter cold winds coming down the Front Range out of Canada, flash flood-inducing rains resulting from monsoon moisture dragged up from the Gulf of Mexico, blizzards, and a variety of other atmospheric phenomena. This evening was a sweet spot.

When the night chill started to settle in, Elsie and I went inside. Elsie laid down next to her food bowl, wanting to be sure I knew it was dinner time. I went into my home office and checked emails. There was one from Veronica saying the Fed chairman's visit to Denver had gone smoothly, with only a smattering of noisy but peaceful protests outside the Denver Federal Reserve Bank. She said she would be coming down to Colorado Springs for a weekend visit and was looking forward to a quiet Saturday but, she said, she'd be up for another fishing adventure on Sunday if I was so inclined. She said she had been in touch with Ed and had offered him a few carefully worded suggestions about investigating Duane's possible drug-related activities and where the internet post accusing Jeff

Freeman of inappropriate behavior involving members of his school's volleyball team might have come from. I sent her a quick reply saying Elsie and I would be eagerly awaiting her arrival.

There was then an email from Charlie Justin. He had met with the attorney representing Jeff Freeman's school district and had assured her a well-publicized lawsuit accusing the school district of breach of contract, abuse of process and other legal sins would be filed "shortly" if she couldn't come up with credible witness statements backing the allegations in the anonymous internet post. I sent Charlie a reply thanking him for his efforts and encouraging him to keep the burners on high while Ed (and Veronica) looked for clues concerning the origin of the internet post.

I then gave Elsie her dinner, fixed myself a salad with some chunks of leftover chicken and watched a couple of innings of the Rockies game where, for a change, they were ahead in a road game, this time in Chicago, against the Cubs. (However, the Rockies bullpen would eventually give up eight runs and lose the game.)

On Thursday, although I was still haunted by RJ's death, I spent some time working on his estate, as I knew he would have wanted me to do. He had nicely set things up so that a probate proceeding would not in fact be necessary. He had recorded a beneficiary deed for his house, causing ownership to transfer to his children equally on his death. His financial accounts were all set up with pay-on-death instructions so his children now also owned the money in those accounts. He had named his children as the beneficiaries of a small life insurance policy and an individual retirement account, so no probate action was necessary there. He had signed a Division of Motor

Vehicles form transferring ownership of the Winnebago at his death to Trout Unlimited, although I doubted Trout Unlimited would have the same fondness for this vehicle that RJ had. This left the disposition of his tangible personal property unresolved, but I knew he wanted me to have his fishing gear and his children to have everything else, and a probate action wouldn't be necessary to achieve any of that.

However, a problem for me, as the personal representative named in RJ's will, was his multiple boxes of client files stored in his basement (some of which had, over the years, been visited by wood rats looking for nest material). Lawyers are supposed to retain client files for ten years after they cease to be active and, even after that, before they are destroyed, clients are supposed to receive a last-chance-to-claim notice. Since RJ had quit the active practice of law five years ago and sorting through his files in order determine to whom such notices should be send would be a major exercise with no benefit to anyone, I decided I would sit tight for a few weeks and then turn all of his files over to a documents shredding company. This might not be quite what the Rules of Professional Conduct had in mind but, since RJ was dead, I saw no reason to think a grievance for inappropriate file destruction presented a threat I should worry about. RJ told me many times the only way to escape from his ethical duty to preserve client files was death, after which he wouldn't care anymore and the problem would be mine. I also wasn't worried, although perhaps I should have been, that one of RJ's clients would come after me as his personal representative for having destroyed a file.

Friday was a catch-up day in the office and I bailed out early, at 4:30. When I got home, Veronica had already made it down from Denver. Her boss let her go home at

2:00 in appreciation for her help protecting the chairman of
the Fed from political damage during his trip to Denver. She
was on the front porch with Elsie by her side. Veronica had
a chardonnay in hand. Elsie had a tennis ball at the ready,
just in case someone wanted to throw it out in the yard for
her to chase. At the moment, that seemed unlikely.

Also, Cooper was in the driveway giving Veronica's
Subaru a wash. He had struck a bargain with her that, if he
washed her car, she would let him use it for a Saturday night
date. Cooper, with his true love Samantha fading (painfully)
in the rear-view mirror, had discovered the girl next door.
Her name was Amy and she had grown up and was no
longer a skinny little thing in pigtails, as he had known her to
be. Showing great courage, he had asked her to go with him
to a movie and, to his considerable relief, she had accepted.
She was heading to the University of Colorado at Boulder in
August and she was eager to debrief Cooper on what life as a
freshman in college, away from home, was all about.

"Cooper," Veronica shouted from the deck, "you
need to work on the wheels. They are covered with brake
dust. And don't forget to vacuum the interior." Cooper
frowned, but went to work on the wheels and pulled an old
vacuum cleaner out of my garage.

When Cooper was finished with the car, and had
done an acceptable job, he helped himself to a beer from my
refrigerator and joined us on the deck.

"Good job, Coop," I said. "Just be sure you don't
try to show Amy what trail braking is all about." This
comment came from an incident a couple of years ago when
Cooper, while driving one of his parents' cars, crashed into a
tree in Monument Valley Park. Samantha was a passenger
and Cooper was trying to demonstrate a race car driver

technique that allows faster exits out of a corner. Samantha ended up in the hospital, although without serious injury. This was partially my fault since I had told Cooper about trail braking when, one day on this very same porch, we had been discussing my days back in California as a reasonably successful amateur sports car racer.

"Right Jack," Cooper said. "I learned my lesson, although I really like the idea of sports car racing. After you teach me fly fishing, can that be the next thing you teach me?"

"I don't believe your financial aid package covers that, but maybe we can go watch a few local amateur races and see what you think."

And then Veronica chimed in. "Cooper, tomorrow, the car will be ready for you, here in the driveway, at 5:00 p.m. And just like a car rental, the gas tank will be full when you pick up the car and it needs to be full when you bring it back. My proof of insurance and registration are in the glove box and be sure you have your driver's license."

"Thanks Veronica. So many rules."

Me: "Get used to it Cooper. That's the way of the world. And Cooper, Veronica and I are going fly fishing on Sunday. Do you want to come along?"

Cooper: "You bet. What time?"

Me: "We'll leave here at 7:00 so don't stay up all night with Amy. Wear long pants and a long sleeve shirt, and bring a wind breaker. We'll be going up to 10,000 feet and it's likely to be chilly. I'll have all the fishing gear you need. Veronica is now a veteran so she can go off on her own. I'll work with you on the basics."

Cooper, knowing this was now expected of him, surrendered his beer can and headed on down the street to his parents' home, leaving Veronica and me to catch up. It had been a challenging week for her with the Fed chairman in town. And I was still reeling from the death of RJ, which I couldn't get out of my mind and couldn't talk about.

"I have enormous respect for the chairman," Veronica told me. "He has a gift for keeping the other members of the board in line and a gift for causing trouble-making Congressmen and Senators to think they are being participatory in the Fed's business but in fact ignoring them when the time comes to make important decisions. But what about RJ?"

"He's been cremated, along with one of his favorite fly rods. I've made arrangements with his two kids to spread his ashes, and Abby's ashes, two weeks from now at the location RJ has chosen, along the bank of the South Platte River at the west end of Eleven Mile Canyon. That's going to be a hard trip for me, but I need to get it behind me. RJ and I often talked about death on our fishing trips and we were in sync that, when the death of a friend or a spouse or a parent or whatever throws you a sharp breaking curve ball, you need to grieve, pick yourself up and march on."

We then headed into the house to feed Elsie and whip up a what-ever-is-in-the-refrigerator salad for ourselves. After dinner, we headed out to my backyard deck to watch the moon rise over Pikes Peak. We shared a two-person deck chair and it felt especially good tonight to have Veronica by my side.

Although I didn't think I'd be in the mood, Veronica convinced me that a snuggle on the deck might be therapeutic. She headed off to the bathroom for a quick shower and came back soft and pink and smelling wonderfully of Shalimar, and wearing a white teddy. The soft light of evening and a rising moon make her glow like a fantasy goddess and I had no resistance to offer. My deck is private other than for an occasional police helicopter overhead -- none on the scene at the moment -- and there was no reason to go back inside. Veronica said, based on a scorecard she apparently kept, that it was a lady's choice night and she wanted me on top. I obliged and we came together in a mix of sexual excitement and emotional catharsis. When we were done, I found myself crying and holding tightly to Veronica (and also thinking my deck furniture was not well designed for this sort of thing).

Chapter 18

Sunday morning, I enticed Veronica out of bed at an early hour with promises of tea. After making it to the kitchen, she continued out to the driveway to confirm that Cooper had returned her Subaru with no obvious signs of damage. While she returned to the kitchen and worked on her tea (and a soggy microwaved croissant I made for her), I loaded fishing gear in my SUV for Veronica, Cooper and me. I then made us some sandwiches for lunch and, when Cooper showed up at the appointed hour, we headed off on our adventure. Before we left, I explained to Elsie that she couldn't go on this trip and reminded her that she had access to my backyard through the doggy door if she needed to go out. Although Fletcher would have taken action to be sure I felt guilty about leaving him behind on a fishing trip, Elsie expressed no such concern.

We went west on Highway 24 up Ute Pass, past the turn off to the Cave of the Winds and, when we got to Divide, we turned south on Highway 67 and headed for Victor, famous as a gold mining hot bed (and a place of labor violence) in the late 1800's, and now surviving as a modestly interesting tourist destination. We then headed back east on a gravel road toward Skagway Reservoir, where we parked and put on waders, wading boots and fishing vests. This took some time since Veronica and Cooper had never worn these items before and putting on wading boots over bulky stocking foot waders took practice. I had already rigged up three fly rods, complete with Adams 12's on the end of 8-foot leaders, so that part of our gear was ready to go.

Our destination for today's fishing was Beaver Creek. Colorado actually has several dozen streams named Beaver Creek. This one begins at the base of the Skagway Reservoir dam and runs downhill in a southerly direction for a distance of maybe fifteen miles where, after numerous irrigation diversions, it empties into the Arkansas River. The first five miles of the creek is in a lush valley with a mixture of high mountain grasses, cottonwoods and ponderosa pines, abundant wildflowers, colorful birds rarely seen at lower elevations, and an occasion moose. Black bears are sometimes in the neighborhood as well but they are mostly shy critters who leave fishermen alone. In this area, the terrain is gentle, as is the current, and the stream is no more than 20 feet wide. Plus, in this area, the banks of the stream are largely free of willows, which makes fly fishing easier.

After the first five miles, however, the creek drops down into a rugged, bolder strewn, canyon. It takes at least two days -- maybe three -- to hike down the entire length of the creek and only well-equipped back backers who, afterwards, like to drink beer and boast about their near-death experience, make the trip. I had never hiked the entire length of the creek but, at least in my younger years, I had always kept this on my list of backcountry journeys I needed to make. In any event, Veronica, Cooper and I were going to stay in the upper meadow area and pursue the small -- mostly eight inch -- brown trout that hang out there and are not too fussy about what they eat.

On the drive to the reservoir, Veronica, after the tea kicked in and her brain came back to life, assumed the role of fishing guide and, even though she had only been fly fishing a couple of times, took it upon herself to explain to Cooper what fly fishing was all about. She was mostly accurate in her presentation and I only occasionally had to add a correction or a comment. Whether Cooper was paying attention was somewhat in doubt. He preferred to talk about his date with Amy, which apparently had gone well, and to look for advice from Veronica and me about what should come next in their relationship.

The three of us headed down a modestly steep, but short, trail to the creek and then walked along a primitive ranch road that borders the creek for another mile. This put us at the spot I had in mind for our fishing. It was a clear sky, 60-degree, morning and our only challenge coming from Mother Nature was a wind that cycled between barely noticeable and 15 m.p.h. Fortunately, the wind was mostly blowing up stream. This helps with fly casting since the wind adds distance to a cast. A downstream wind does exactly the opposite and contributes to knots in the leader, flies penetrating ear lobes and other distractions. Casting upstream is important because trout look upstream for food carried in the current. They don't look downstream to see if they are being stalked by wily predators wearing waders and boots.

In an effort to demonstrate what we would be doing, I waded out into the middle of the stream, made a few casts and actually caught a fish, which stoked my self-esteem and Cooper's confidence that I knew what I was doing. I scooped the little guy up into my net and promptly released it, an easy act since we were using barbless hooks. I took this opportunity to reinforce the lesson that fish should be handled as little as possible, not played to exhaustion, and quickly released once they appeared to be breathing normally.

I then sent Veronica downstream maybe fifty yards to fend for herself, with instructions to yell if she needed help, and started working with Cooper. I assisted him in wading into the middle of the stream and to make a cast, telling him to use more wrist than arm. His first few tries at this were clumsy but then he seemed to get the idea that he was using the fly rod to throw the line and his casts improved. However, on about his fourth cast, he managed to snag a clump of grass growing by the side of the stream and we had to move up to a spot I thought had probably been holding fish in order to free the fly. This, of course, sent the fish racing upstream. On maybe his fifteenth cast, Cooper caught a fish -- a six-inch brown trout -- and reeled it in, to be netted and released. He was ecstatic and no doubt concluded he was a fly fishing natural, on his way to the fly fishing hall of fame. But, this euphoria was short lived since, immediately thereafter, Cooper slipped on a rock and fell into the stream. I, as someone with experience at this, helped him back up, brushed off some of the water, told him this was part of the sport, and put him back to work in pursuit of trout.

After an hour of fishing, I called a time out and we ate the lunch I had brought by the side of the stream. Veronica reported she had caught "at least" eight fish all by herself and had also apparently concluded she deserved to be in the fly fishing hall of fame. Amazingly enough, her Adams 12 was still intact and ready to take on further gullible fish.

After our lunch, we fished for another forty-five minutes or so, working our way up stream toward the dam.

We all caught a few more fish, but the action seemed to have slowed from the time we first started fishing.

We were marching right along back toward the dam when I suddenly heard Veronica say: "Oh my God, what is that?" What had grabbed Veronica's attention was a large bull moose, standing directly in our path.

"OK everyone, stay quiet and stay still," I said, with my best command voice. "These guys are usually not aggressive but you never know. Let's just move slowly around him as far to the right as we can get. If he decides to charge, I'll get him to come after me and you two hustle on up the road."

The moose didn't charge, continued eating willows, and paid no attention to us as we passed. But, it was still a noteworthy experience and Cooper couldn't resist turning it into a photo opportunity with his cell phone camera, no doubt thinking Amy would be impressed with his bravery.

At the foot of the dam, where the creek begins, there is a nice pond which sometimes holds larger fish. We stopped to fish there for a few minutes and I hooked up with a rare fourteen incher. Veronica and Cooper, however, spooked the remaining fish in the pond and caught nothing.

We were back at my SUV by 2:00, stripped off our gear, and headed home. There was, at first, nonstop chatter about how much fun we had had but then, once we were on a smooth paved road, there was silence since Veronica and Cooper both fell asleep.

Back at my place, Elsie greeted us with a three-on-a-scale-of-ten tail wag from her dog bed. Cooper and Veronica helped me put away the fishing gear. I let Cooper keep one of the fly rods so he could practice casting in his front yard (and maybe induce a visit from Amy, allowing him to show off his newly acquired hunter/gather skills). Cooper said thanks for his first ever lesson in fly fishing, urged me to follow up with a fly-tying lesson, gave Veronica back her key fob for the Subaru, showed her his debit card receipt for a gas purchase and headed home. Veronica packed up her luggage (again enough for a world cruise), gave me a wonderful kiss and hug, and took off for Denver, knowing she would have an unpleasant and slow-going slog through the Sunday afternoon I-25 traffic and through the Gap, the never-ending construction project between Monument Hill and Castle Rock that generates something like 800 accidents a year.

I popped open a beer and took it out to the front porch where I tried, unsuccessfully, to think useful thoughts about what to do next to help Scott dig out from the stress I knew was increasing with every passing day. Elsie, in due course, joined me on the porch and put her head in my lap, which always made me feel better about just about everything.

Chapter 19

On Monday afternoon, I received a call from Jocelyn Alvarez, Attorney Regulation Counsel. She said she had received Scott's response to the grievance Duane Thurston had filed and wanted to, informally, talk about this case. Such ex parte -- one side only -- discussions with the person who prosecutes attorney grievances is apparently permitted and I tried to answer her questions as best I could. I was not able to pick up any signals from her as to how she might be seeing things. She seemed to be hanging up, as Duane Thurston had hoped, on the idea that, by representing the trustee of a trust, a lawyer somehow owed duties to the beneficiaries of the trust. I told her I understood the issue but that, after diligent research (done mostly by Scott's office, although I didn't tell her that...), I had not found any appellate court cases in Colorado, or elsewhere, that spoke to the matter. I took the opportunity to again pitch the idea that trustees need to be able to engage lawyers who represent them and who can give them independent legal advice without worrying about conflicts of interest involving beneficiaries. To be expected, there was no comment from Ms. Alvarez on this topic. She said she would discuss the matter with her staff and then decide if the grievance needed to be moved upstream to the Attorney Regulation Committee, which could decide to dismiss the grievance or conduct a hearing. In all events, whatever decision the Committee finally reached would be presented to the Presiding Disciplinary Judge, who would have the final say. There wasn't anything more for me to do on this front other than check in with Scott and give him a status report. He again sounded tired and showed no interest in spending time talking about the grievance or where it was headed. I knew his firm's management committee was aware of the grievance but didn't seem overly concerned, as long as Scott was continuing to generate the income the firm had come to expect from him and the many other lawyers who worked under him.

On Tuesday afternoon, Ed checked in. He was out of the poker tournament, having lost all the money the casino had fronted him and some of his own. The lone woman participant in the tournament, a regular at these events (referred to by the other participants behind her back as Shark Face) held the ultimate winning hand -- four kings -- and walked off with everyone else's chips. This meant Ed's free room and board was over, so he was back in his bus and headed to his favorite hangout along the California coast north of San Francisco, in the general vicinity of Point Reyes.

"Hi Jack. Not much to report but, with help from some colleagues in my business who shall remain nameless, I have picked up on a few scents I'm starting to explore. Although Duane Thurston has done a very good job of hiding his activities, I have reason to believe he may in fact be a participant, although perhaps a minor one, in a complex and large criminal enterprise that sells narcotic prescription pain medicines on the street. I'm trying to learn more about the distribution network and work my way back through the supply chain. These drugs are, of course, tightly controlled because they are dangerous and addictive. They legitimately move from manufacturers to middlemen drug brokers and on to pharmacies and hospitals and health care providers, and records are kept every step of the way. The middlemen brokers, called in polite circles 'pharmacy benefit managers,' are a big player on this stage and are mostly regulated at the state level, which means not regulated very much. My guess is they are the weak link in the supply chain, most vulnerable to leaks. My current theory is that this criminal enterprise has figured out a way to divert drugs out of the supply chain and then market them on the street to addicts who can no longer get the drugs they crave with a prescription. There's lots of money being moved around by this enterprise using Bitcoins, which criminals like because tracing Bitcoin transactions is way harder than tracing other money transactions in the traditional banking system. But, thanks to some really good work by a couple of computer jocks at the Office of the Comptroller of the Currency, there may now be ways to identify the destination of Bitcoin transfers. This knowledge was recently used to recapture a large amount of money paid as a ransom following a ransomware attack on a big East Coast pipeline company. You may have read about this. The attack shut down the availability of gasoline along the whole East Coast, all the way from New Jersey to Florida, for several days."

"Not to meddle or anything, but shouldn't this information be turned over the Food and Drug Administration or the Drug Enforcement Agency or the FBI or the CIA or some politician running for reelection?"

"No. The bad actors would learn about that -- they have lookouts everywhere -- and they would disappear faster than prairie dogs seeing a coyote. We just need to keep scratching around low key and trying to connect vague little dots. In fine mafia style, this operation is undoubtedly structured in a way where no one player, except at the very top, knows the identity of any other player."

"So what's your time line for this project? I have a trial coming up in a few weeks in Texas, where Duane Thurston may have a home field advantage. And Scott Freeman seems to be doing a poor job of coping with stress."

"Jack, it's hard to tell. I'm looking for a home run hour but it could be several weeks before I have one. Even if we learn more about the structure of this criminal enterprise, we still need to figure out how Duane Thurston connects to it."

"And what about the social media defamation attack aimed at Jeff Freeman, Scott's son? Anything to report there?"

"With some off-the-record help from Veronica using tools in her toolbox at the Fed, I've worked my way back one step in the trail of the social media post that accused Jeff of inappropriate behavior with members of his school's volleyball team. But, as I told you before, that post went through multiple check points at different cloud storage companies and it was encrypted every step of the way, using different encryption systems. So it's slow going. I'm going to move in a different direction and do some internet crawling for information from members of the volleyball team who might be gossiping about other members of the team. It's been a long time since I was in high school, but I remember gossiping was a highly refined activity among teenage girls, able to move large amounts of mostly unreliable information along at the speed of light. Social media has greatly enhanced gossiping."

"Well, keep digging and I'll tell Scott we're on our game plan and making progress."

On Wednesday, I did some bona fide lawyer work drafting a motion in the Thurston v. Freeman case. This motion asked Judge Elefson, not to decide the case in total, but to rule on a question of law. Judges rarely grant motions for summary judgment which fully decide a case. They cop out by saying there must be unresolved issues of fact running around somewhere and therefore there needs to be a trial to resolve the issues of fact -- motion denied. However, judges have less trouble ruling on a discrete question of law, which doesn't decide the case but can have a major impact on the outcome of a case.

Lots of lawyers don't seem to get this, but lawsuits consist of issues of fact and issues of law. And, in most lawsuits involving money, it usually turns out that the facts are really not in dispute. What's in dispute is what the law says should be the outcome of the case when rules of law are applied to facts. In other words, facts plus law equals verdict. So, if you can pin down your judge on an important issue of law in your favor, and you know what the facts are finally going to sort out to be, you're in a good position to negotiate a settlement or win a case at trial. If you get the answer you want to a question of law, that answer will roll into the jury instructions at the end of the case.

The lawsuit against Scott was looking like a law case and not a fact case. The facts were not in dispute. Scott represented Maria when she was the trustee of the Thurston Family Trust. He advised her, at her request, that she could amend the trust agreement to reduce the distribution going to Duane and Billie. After she decided that's what she wanted to do, Scott, at Maria's request, prepared the amendment. He did not advise Maria, because she never asked, that she might have a duty to notify Duane and Billie she was amending the trust agreement to their detriment. He also never coached her to reduce the distributions coming to Duane and Billie.

In any event, the motion I was drafting would ask Judge Elefson to rule that a lawyer representing a trustee did not have a duty to advise the beneficiaries of a trust what the trustee was up to and that doing so would in fact be a violation of the duty a lawyer owes to a client to maintain client confidences. In my motion, I was able to reference all manner of cases dealing with the attorney-client privilege. But, as I had told Jocelyn Alvarez, Attorney Regulation Counsel, there don't seem to be any cases around discussing the issue of a lawyer's possible duty to trust beneficiaries when representing a trustee. If I could get Judge Elefson to rule, as a matter of law, that lawyers representing trustees do not thereby owe duties to the beneficiaries of a trust, Duane Thurston's claim against Scott would take a big hit.

There is, of course, a risk in filing a motion requesting a ruling on a question of law. The judge could issue a ruling that is the complete opposite of the ruling you were looking for. Thus, in Scott's case, the judge could rule that a lawyer representing a trustee does in fact have a duty of disclosure running to the trust beneficiaries. Laying the facts in our case on top of such a ruling would be a serious blow to our team seeing as how Scott never told Duane and Billie that Maria, as the trustee of the Thurston Family Trust, was giving them a haircut.

I sent Scott a draft of the motion, explained to him the risk of a backfire, and asked his consent to file the motion. He gave me a green light and I had Stephanie file the motion.

Chapter 20

The call from Stella, Scott's wife, hit my cell phone at 4:34 a.m. on Friday and pulled me out of a mostly peaceful sleep -- hard to come by these days. "Jack, I think Scott has had a heart attack. He started complaining about chest pains and his breathing got short and irregular and his pulse began racing and he started sweating like crazy. In typical guy fashion, he told me it must be something he ate and not to worry but, as I regularly do, I ignored him and called 911. The ambulance picked him up five minutes ago and he's on his way to Penrose Hospital. I also called Rollie Dumbarton and he's headed to the hospital as well. Rollie said he'd be sure they stabilized Scott and he would then have him admitted, and get him out from under the craziness of the emergency room. He said he'd go to work on a diagnosis and treatment plan as soon as the cardiologist on call can get to the hospital and look him over."

"Thanks Stella. You did things just right. I guess I'm not surprised at this. As you know, the Thurston Family Trust situation has been really hard on Scott. Lawyers aren't used to getting sued for representing a client in what they believe, correctly in this case, to be a diligent and proper manner. I'll head over to the hospital and catch up with Rollie. Under patient confidentiality rules -- mainly the Health Insurance Portability and Accountability Act, HIPPA -- nobody is supposed to tell me anything about Scott's condition but I don't think Rollie will decide he can't talk to me because Congress said he shouldn't."

"Thanks Jack. I'm so grateful for your help and friendship. Scott has told me many times how much he appreciates your seeing him through his little skirmishes with people caught up in the throes of death and taxes, and the fumblings of the judicial system. He always puts on a stoic I-can-handle-this front, but in reality he can't. He keeps wanting a perfect world and it's not there. He should have been an ornithologist or something -- not a lawyer."

"I'll check in as soon as I know more."

I threw on an old pair of jeans and a senior softball t-shirt, gave Elsie a dog treat and told her I'd be back for her breakfast as soon as I could, and headed out to the hospital which, this time of day, was a mere ten minutes away. I hadn't been in an emergency room for a while, not since Cooper tried to show Samantha how trail braking worked and hit a tree in Monument Valley Park. The emergency room was, as I suppose it should be, an organized form of chaos, with victims of gunshot wounds, stabbings, domestic violence, drug overdoses, traffic accidents and cardiovascular events all commingled in a relatively small space. The waiting room was filled with concerned friends and family members, who were paying no attention to the TV screens and reading material meant to occupy their time. There were also two armed police officers who, presumably, had an interest in a patient having nothing to do with friends or family.

I managed to talk my way past the sentries whose job it was to keep people like me out of the area where the work was going on. I did this by explaining I was Dr. Dumbarton's lawyer and he had asked me to meet him here. I flashed my Supreme Court attorney registration card at the primary gate keeper and, even though this looks mostly like

a Sam's Club membership card, it seemed to carry some
weight. In any event, I was allowed to go into the space
where the patients were being triaged and found Rollie.

"Hi Jack. Thanks for coming. Scott kept asking me
if you were going to show up and protect him from the
health care conspiracy."

"How's he doing? What's up?"

"He has serious vascular blockages, thanks to a
lifetime of stress, no exercise and exacting ingredients
martinis, all the things I've been telling him he needed to
change. In any event, the on-call cardiologist has, after a
couple of tests and with the help of one of his heart surgeon
colleagues, teed up Scott for a quadruple bypass surgery
tomorrow morning. There is no time to waste on something
like this. Otherwise, permanent damage can result. I know
the doc who's going to do the surgery and she's good. She
trained at Mayo and moved here so she could ski more. If I
ever need heart surgery, she'd be my choice."

"Can I see Scott?"

"He's sedated at the moment so, no."

"What are the odds of his coming through this OK?
And what's involved in the recovery?

"He should come through the surgery OK since he
doesn't have any other serious health conditions --
morbidities we call them in the medical profession in order
to sound important. But the recovery is going to be tough --
at least a month before he can do much of anything useful
and another month after that before he can go back to work
at his office."

"He, of course, will try to be back at his desk by
Monday but I'll get Stella geared up to reign him in and
maybe find him some nice online chess tournaments he can

plug into or a Netflix subscription or something. As you
recall, Scott was the Colorado state chess champion for
several years until some twelve-year old girl knocked him
off his perch. And I'll get Scott's secretary and the
managing partner at his firm to be sure his clients are taken
care of. When he wakes up from the surgery, that's going to
be his number one worry. Also, as you know, one of the big
stresses in his life these days is that he's being sued by an
unhappy trust beneficiary who is trying to blame him for a
reduction in the distribution he is going to receive from a
trust. This is basically extortion by litigation but the lawsuit
has enough traction to hang a cloud over Scott's head. The
case is actually set for a trial in Texas in a few weeks.
Although I'd like to march full speed ahead to get this matter
out of Scott's life, I may have to ask for a continuance
because of his medical condition."

"As soon as I know more, I'll give you a call. I'll
also give Stella a call as soon as I get back to my office. If
you can follow up and keep her informed and under control,
that would be great. It would help me a lot if she can dump
some of her anxieties on you rather than me. I have a full
schedule in my office the next couple of days. You and
Scott aren't the only old people I have to take care of. But
I'll be in regular touch with the hospital and I'll let you
know what I hear. They'll be moving Scott into a hospital
room shortly, on the cardiac patient wing of the third floor.
You may be able to talk with him tomorrow morning, and
with the surgeon -- her name is Brianna McMann -- before
they wheel him off to the surgery unit."

"Thanks Rollie."

"Oh, and Jack, if you get to talk to Scott, will you
please tell him I had my colonoscopy? It wasn't as awful as

I had imagined and I don't have colon cancer, which is a relief. I still fart a lot but no one seems to be too concerned about that except maybe my wife."

Since there wasn't anything more for me to do at the hospital, I headed back home and gave Elsie her breakfast. I then called Stella. She had already talked with Rollie so she basically knew what was happening. I told her I would cycle back to her with any information coming my way. And I called Veronica to tell her about Scott's heart attack. When she didn't answer my call, I sent her a text message telling her about Scott's condition. (Sending text messages is still problematic for me since I have been unsuccessful training my thumbs in the necessary keystrokes. But, with hunting and pecking, I can still get the job done.) It was then into the shower and off to the office to deal with a long list of matters where a friend's heart attack had not been part of the day's plan.

Over the noon hour, I managed to get in a trip to the Y and a jog in the park, which helped to calm me down about Scott's condition. After my jog, I took another quick shower and decided it was time for a weigh in. I was glad to see I was holding my own at 180 pounds, although I wasn't entirely pleased with the distribution of those pounds. But, when I looked around the locker room, it was clear to me I was doing better than many of my peers.

And, Friday was a senior softball night, which again helped me take my mind off Scott being locked up in a hospital and teed up for a complex surgery the next day. I had played softball with the same bunch of guys for a decade and, since there was now a separate league for players 60 and over, I, at age 60, was one of the kids on my team. Senior softball brings together people from all walks of life.

My team, named the Hoot Owls -- don't ask me why -- has a just-retired four star general, an orthopedic surgeon (very useful for people playing senior softball), a high school basketball coach, two Fed Ex truck drivers, an accountant and a still competing professional bull rider whose body consists largely of after-market parts but who can hit a softball a long way.

One of the benefits of playing senior softball is the substantial amount of medical information that ends up being exchanged. There is a regular and thoughtful dialogue about which nonsteroidal anti-inflammatory over the counter drugs provide the best relief for aching muscles, joints, tendons, etc. And, the competence of local massage therapists is reviewed weekly.

I was assigned the position of third base for this season, which has proven to be challenging -- and dangerous. But so far, the putouts have exceeded the errors and my only injuries have been bruises to my shins. (I have learned the wisdom of getting out of the way when a scorching line drive is headed toward me.) In tonight's game, I managed two bloop singles and two fly outs -- no strike outs -- and made two putouts on defense so, as such things go, it was a good night. I declined the opportunity to join my teammates after the game for an adult beverage at the Squatting Chicken sports bar across the street from the ball field and headed home to give Elsie a late dinner and a final visit to the front yard fire hydrant.

Scott's surgery -- a quadruple bypass -- was scheduled for 8:00 a.m. on Saturday. I was at the hospital at 6:00 and had a chance to talk with Scott for a few minutes before they started giving him drugs and attaching him to various machines. He was groggy but generally in good spirits.

"Thanks for coming Jack. I'll get through this just fine. They know I'm a lawyer so they'll be especially careful. Please take care of Stella while I'm -- uh -- away, and my clients. And do whatever you think you need to do to keep Duane Thurston at bay."

"Not to worry. Everything is under control and, no offense, but the world will hardly miss you while you're recovering. Oh, and Rollie told me to tell you he had his colonoscopy, it wasn't as bad as he thought, and he doesn't have colon cancer. So he says, under the terms of your bet with him, the ball is now in your court."

"The bastard. Here I am about to have my chest cracked open and he wants to gloat about our bet."

At that point, Dr. McMann popped into the room -- a perky 5-foot four-inch blond who was probably fifty years old but looked thirty. I introduced myself as Scott's lawyer and, ignoring HIPPA, she explained how Scott's arteries were plugged up and were limiting blood flow to his heart. He had not had a full-blown heart attack, where his heart quit working. But, he was right on the edge of that and without the surgery it would happen. She said she had spoken with Stella and given her this same information.

"With this surgery," Dr. McMann said, "we basically redo the plumbing that brings blood to the heart and, as long as he behaves himself after the surgery, the threat of a widow maker heart attack is greatly reduced. Thirty years ago, this kind of surgery was science fiction. Now it's routine. There's still plenty of risk but the risks of the procedure outweigh the risks of not treating the arterial blockages. Bottom line, we've learned to do this procedure with, for the most part, good outcomes."

"So what can I do to help?"

"What you've already done. Be his friend. Let him know lots of people really care about him. Try to control the stress in his life, to the extent you can. During the recovery period, while he still remembers what it's like to have his chest cut open, get him to clean up his act with regard to diet, exercise and alcohol."

"Thanks doctor. Scott is a remarkable person and is what all lawyers should try to be. We need him back in action. Do your best work. Lots of people are counting on you." She smiled and left the room.

I was then told by a don't-mess-with-me kind of nurse that it was time to leave and Scott was wheeled away toward the operating theater, with multiple tubes coming out of bottles on hangers connected to his body.

I went home and took Elsie for a long walk up into Pike National Forest, which abuts my neighborhood on the west side. The effects of the drought we were experiencing were not yet evident and the birds I normally see in the spring were flying around and, with their calls, announcing their interest in bird sex. Elsie enjoyed these walks and dutifully staked out her territory, picking her spots in a thoughtful manner. We worked our way past one skunk parked in the middle of the trail and let the squirrels make their rounds, although Elsie let me know she thought they deserved a good chase.

Rollie called me on my cell about 11:30. The surgery had gone as planned, with no surprises. Scott was in recovery and coming out of the anesthesia. The way they do things these days, he would likely be up and walking the halls of the hospital in a few hours, and I would be able to pay him a short visit at around 4:00. Rollie said he had already called Stella and given her this report. I then called Stella and invited her to meet me at the hospital at 4:15 to see Scott.

Stella and I met in the hospital lobby, dutifully wearing masks as still required because of the COVID pandemic. We announced our purpose to the person manning the check-in desk, were given badges and told we could proceed up to the seventh floor where Scott's room was located. After exiting the elevator, we were greeted by one of the nurses manning the seventh-floor nursing station. She told us Scott was in room 715 and the door should be open. She cautioned us that we could spend no more than 15 minutes with him since he was pretty beat up by the day's events and needed to rest.

Scott was dozing when we entered the room and looking pale. He was attached to two IV's. One was a saline solution to keep him hydrated. The other was a pain medication drip which he was allowed, within reason, to control. Stella, who was by now crying, kissed him on the forehead, which brought him out of his doze.

"Well hello Stella. Hello Jack," he said with a weak smile. "I guess they didn't kill me. The doctor said I did great, although I don't know what that means and it may just be marketing. They let me get up and walk around for a few minutes, and let me pee, although that proved to be challenging."

Rollie showed up shortly after we did and provided us with some further medical information. The surgery had accomplished its purpose of improving blood flow to Scott's heart. Dr. McMann also told Rollie there was too much plaque in Scott's arteries and he would need to start using a daily medicine to keep that under control. Otherwise, he could still be a candidate for a heart attack or a stroke. Dr. McMann told Rollie that Scott had tolerated the anesthesia well and, as such things go, the surgery had been routine. If all went as planned, he would be able to go home in five days and begin his at-home recovery. A physical therapist from the hospital would accompany him on the trip home and give him further discharge instructions, to include a schedule of light exercise, which would mostly involve walking.

"So Jack, what's happening at my office?"

"They're on top of this. Everything on your calendar has been assigned to another lawyer and your assistant, Shelley, is handling your email and mail and keeping everything organized. Oh, and she cancelled your filling replacement dental appointment for next week. She thought you might want to wait on that."

"And what about Thurston?"

"Duane's lawyer filed a response to my motion for an order on a question of law. Not surprisingly, he pitched the idea that my motion presented a mixed question of fact and law, so the judge couldn't give the ruling I requested until the facts were fully determined, meaning a trial. I'll file a reply brief reminding the judge that my motion told him to assume all of the facts in the case were what Duane's lawyer was claiming them to be. But, we may get hometowned on this one."

"And what about Jeff?"

"Ed says he's making progress figuring out who originated the social media post that slammed Jeff and caused him to be pulled out of the classroom and sidelined as the coach of the volleyball team. Jeff's lawyer from his teacher's union is making the appropriate threats to the school district, through its lawyer. Jeff, as you might expect, since he has your DNA, is frustrated by these events but his wife, although she is dealing with her own stress, has kept him under control and convinced him that he should use this as an opportunity to work in his garden and go fishing more."

"And the grievance?"

"No word there. I sent the Attorney Regulation Counsel our motion for a ruling on a question of law that we filed in the Texas case since that question -- a lawyer's legal duties to trust beneficiaries -- is front and center in the grievance. I don't expect to hear anything back from her for a couple of weeks. Her office is apparently not known for expeditious processing."

At this point, our time with Scott was up and he was showing well-earned signs of fatigue. So, Rollie and I shook Scott's extended hand and Stella gave him another kiss -- this time on the mouth -- and we headed out.

Chapter 21

I went directly home from the hospital and found Veronica and Elsie on the front porch. Veronica had decided, at the last minute, that she would spend the weekend with us, although her work was piling up back in Denver thanks to shifting political sands at the Federal Reserve Board and continuing reports of foreign agents hacking into U.S. government networks that were supposed to be bullet proof secure.

After a kiss and a hug from Veronica, and a tail wag from Elsie, I grabbed a beer out of the refrigerator, which is what Veronica was drinking, and joined them on the porch.

"What's the news on Scott?"

"He came through the surgery OK -- no surprises, the doctor said. Stella and I, and Rollie, visited with him for maybe fifteen minutes before they chased us out of his room. He's obviously tired and his brain is fuzzed from the narcotic pain medicine they are letting him drip into his body, but he was coherent enough to want to know how things were going back at his office and what was happening on the Thurston Family Trust front. The nurse on duty told us she thought he'd be able to go home in another four days and begin his at-home recovery protocol."

"That all sounds good."

"Yes, but I hope he finally gets the message that he needs some lifestyle changes. Like diligent exercise and no more martinis if he doesn't want to have his chest cracked open again."

"And what about you, my love? How are you holding up?"

"Veronica, lawyers who do what I do for a living are trained in the art of stress management, so I'm OK. But I'm unhappy how the world is beating up on Scott and I'm unhappy that we have lost RJ. It has occurred to me that, with RJ gone, other than you and Elsie and Scott and Cooper, I don't really have many friends. My law partners are great and so are my office staff and so are the senior softball guys, but the words business colleagues and teammates, more than friends, seem to better describe those relationships."

"So why don't you join a service club or a fishing club or take up golf or do something that will cause you to crawl out from your misanthropic rabbit hole and make friends? Maybe even hang out at a church. Guys are so weird about this stuff."

"Well, thanks for the counsel Veronica. But maybe because law school and the legal profession have diminished my ability to trust very many people, I have found that, for the most part, I prefer dogs to people, other than you of course, and I really like my time alone on a trout stream, matching wits with fish rather than lawyers or judges."

"It's part of your charm, Jack. But listen, I have something I need to talk with you about. There's a guy in my office -- his name is Jerry -- who I think is hitting on me. He's another computer jock at the Fed but with assignments different from mine. He's not my boss but he reports to my boss, so I guess we have equal rank in the tribe. In any event, for the last few weeks he's been making occasional complimentary comments about my hair and my clothes. And earlier this week, he needed to see something on my computer screen and, while looking at my screen from behind me, he put his hands on my shoulders. It felt really creepy. Under the Fed's sexual harassment policy, I should probably report his conduct to the person who is supposed to be in charge of this sort of thing, but I don't want to get this guy in trouble. And, I don't want to get myself in trouble for not reporting his behavior. And so, bottom line, I don't know what to do."

"As someone who remembers looking over your shoulder at a computer screen when we were working on the S.O.S. case, and thereafter falling in love with you, I can understand how this might happen. And I give Jerry credit for good taste. But, what to do. Here's my vote. You talk to him and tell him you find his conduct unwelcome and problematic. Plant the threat, politely, that you may have to turn him in to the sexual harassment police if he doesn't back off. And then you watch to see what happens. Hopefully, that will be the end of the matter."

"That's where I landed but I needed a second opinion."

"I have to say, Veronica, I find this whole 'me too' thing incomprehensible. Women spend billions of dollars a year trying to make themselves sexually attractive to men and, when it works and men are in fact attracted, they sue them. Maybe this is just arrogance on my part, but I've always thought you might have taken extra measures to make yourself sexually attractive to me. If so, it has certainly worked, and I hope you're keep it up and you're not planning to sue me."

Veronica, in an effort to move the conversation in a slightly different direction, said: "The real problem, of course, is when men in positions of power and authority

demand sexual favors in exchange for promotions or
employment opportunities, things like that. Otherwise, I
think women's behavior, and men's response, is built into
the DNA. All animals are designed to propagate their
species and, in that regard, humans are no different than, say,
hummingbirds -- or trout."

"Whatever. In all events, I'd just suggest you tell
Jerry you're accounted for, and to back off."

"Will do. But to be sure I understand your position
on this, can you put your hands on my shoulders?"

We had a quiet dinner on the deck, watching the
stars and planets come to life over Pikes Peak, and then it
was early to bed, after a last trip for Elsie to the fire hydrant
at the end of the driveway, with a good night's sleep the only
agenda.

Veronica headed back to Denver on Sunday
morning. I then paid a brief visit to Scott at the hospital -- he
was doing OK but still had lots of pain from the trauma of
the surgery and seemed modestly buzzed from the pain
medication. After that I headed to my office to catch up on
neglected work. I found there the reply Manifort had filed to
my motion for a ruling on a question of law. As expected,
he tried to blunt the risk my motion created by arguing that
the question I had asked the court to answer was not purely a
question of law. It was a mixed question of fact and law,
and therefore the judge couldn't answer the question without
a trial to finally sort out all disputed questions fact. I
whipped out a reply brief, which I was allowed to do as the
party filing the motion, saying the question I had presented
to the court in my motion assumed that all issues of fact
were to be resolved as Manifort's client said they should be
resolved. So, there was no need for a trial in order to answer

my question of law. But, I was not optimistic Judge Elefson would toss me the bone I was looking for. In a civil dispute, trial court judges try not to decide anything they don't have to in the hope the case will settle and they won't need to rule on something that might lead to a reversal at the court of appeals -- a black mark on their score card.

Chapter 22

Tuesday was the day RJ's children -- daughter Becky and son David -- and I had agreed we would deposit RJ's and Abby's ashes at the spot RJ had selected, at the west end of Eleven Mile Canyon. After giving the matter considerable thought, Becky and David had decided RJ's grandchildren should not come along, since they were still too young to understand what we were up to.

The location RJ had chosen is where the South Platte River empties out of Eleven Mile Reservoir on its way to Denver and forms a picture-perfect, and entomologically perfect, trout stream. The canyon is narrow in most places, with colorful rock walls on both sides, but it occasionally opens up into meadows where whitetail deer, elk and an occasional moose hang out, and where abundant wildflowers find a home. There are a couple of one-way tunnels halfway up the canyon drilled out of granite requiring caution. Fly fishermen come from around the world to test their skills in Eleven Mile Canyon. And the fish are up to the challenge. They have seen it all and know the difference between a real bug and a manmade imitation. So a fisherman, to be successful here, must practice stealth and has to know how to precisely place an artificial fly in the current in just such a way that it imitates the behavior of a real insect. And, these fish limit their diet to only very small flies, adding further to the fisherman's challenge (especially those of us with older eyes). RJ was a master at fishing the canyon and I have no doubt the fish feared him, although he always used barbless hooks, never played a fish to exhaustion, and promptly returned the fish he caught to the river after having taught them to be careful what they eat.

Since I knew the way and had a season pass into the canyon, where a fee is charged for access, Becky and David drove down from Denver to Colorado Springs and I drove from there. The drive, which was a little more than an hour, gave us a chance to talk about RJ's life, allowing me to learn things about his life he had never shared with me. He grew up as an only child in a small town in central Kansas, where his mother and father were both lawyers. They were country lawyers, meaning they did whatever needed to be done to help their clients, and meaning trust, humility, compassion and respect were more important than detailed knowledge of rules of law. They also owned and operated a small farm producing vegetables that regularly won awards at the county fair. The farm additionally supported a few head of cattle and a dozen or so goats. When he was growing up, and during summers when he was in college and law school, RJ put in time working on his parents' farm. RJ, I learned, was also an outstanding high school football player -- a running back -- which won him a scholarship to the University of Kansas, where he excelled at that position until his left knee was destroyed by a cataclysmic and illegal tackle.

When we made it to the west end of the canyon, we parked my SUV and divided RJ's ashes into three parts, with Becky, David and I each taking a share. I kept Abby's ashes. We then went off in different directions allowing each of us to have our own private thoughts about RJ's life and death. I went down stream a quarter of a mile to a part of the river with lots of structure and where RJ would regularly find the largest fish in the canyon. I spread my share of his ashes, and Abby's ashes, partly along the bank and partly in the water. At this location, there were several trout grazing on small bluewing olive mayflies that had hatched out of their nymphal form and were floating in the surface foam. Easy pickings for the fish. The fish would have been easy pickings for RJ.

Silly though it was, I made a little speech to the fish. "OK guys, you're now sharing the river with the soul of a really special guy. You may have thought of him as a predator, but he did more than anyone I know to be sure your home here is protected from development and pollution and overfishing, allowing you to live a happy life and raise your families. His name is RJ Conover and he misses you."

I watched the fish for a few minutes, revisited painful thoughts about my decision not to pull RJ out of his vehicle while he still had a pulse, and then headed back to the SUV, where Becky and David were waiting.

"Jack," Becky said, "this is a beautiful spot. I can see why RJ loved it here and chose this as his final resting place. Thanks for bringing us up here and sharing in this moment."

Without further meaningful conversation, we headed back down the canyon and on to Colorado Springs, where Becky and David got into David's car and took off for their homes in Denver. I sat on the front porch of my home for an hour thinking about life and death -- mostly death -- until the evening chill chased me inside. Elsie stayed with me on the porch, head in my lap, but, as the temperature dropped, she let me know it was dinner time.

Wednesday morning, I stopped by the hospital to see how Scott was doing, and if they were going to let him go home today. The report from the nurses wasn't what I had hoped. Scott's blood pressure had been bouncing around in an erratic manner and a small area along the incision on the left side of his chest was showing signs of a possible infection. So, Scott was stuck in the hospital for at least one more day, and maybe longer. And -- surprise -- he was not happy about this and was convinced the hospital was thinking up excuses to keep him around in pursuit of enhanced revenue.

Rollie showed up while I was there and tried to assure Scott his extended hospital stay was medically indicated. "Bullshit Rollie. This is revenue enhancement, pure and simple. Maybe I'll call my health insurance company and tell them they're getting fleeced by this greedy hospital."

"But Scott," Rollie calmy replied, "if you did that, the amount of time you would spend on hold waiting to find someone to talk to would probably exceed the additional time you're going to be in the hospital."

Since this was a winning argument, Scott backed off, but not before taking a pass at me about arranging an escape. I told him I'd love to help but I felt this would be adverse to his interest in obtaining a dismissal of the grievance filed against him now pending at the Office of Attorney Regulation Counsel, where his overall character and good behavior were in play. And, my helping him escape from a hospital where highly qualified medical professionals had decided he should stay awhile longer could very well result in a disciplinary sanction against me, for aiding and abetting his escape. Fortunately, Stella showed up at this point and her taking charge of the situation (she who must be obeyed...) gave me a chance to slip out the door and head to my office.

Chapter 23

Along with several modestly out of control other matters, I had two Scott-related items on my to-do list for the day -- look for an expert witness to help us in the Texas lawsuit Duane Thurston had brought against Scott, and review the list of possible mediators Manifort had given me. Silvia Everson, our local Texas counsel, recommended to me as an expert witness a woman named Regina Ramirez. She is a tenured professor at the University of Texas law school, teaching courses relating to probate and estate planning. Prior to that, she was head of the trust department of the largest independent bank in Dallas and prior to that she was an estate planning lawyer with a well-respected Texas law firm. I put in a call to Ms. Ramirez and left her a short voice mail message. She returned my call later in the day and I briefly explained to her what the lawsuit Duane Thurston had filed against Scott was all about. Without prodding on my part, she quickly came to the conclusion that this was a lawsuit short on merit. Trustees, she felt, needed to be able to have independent legal representation without trust beneficiaries being able to meddle in the attorney-client relationship. And, once Scott became the successor trustee at Marie's death, he was obligated to administer the trust in accordance with the trust agreement, as Marie had amended it, including Duane's and Billie's haircut. Scott, as trustee, had no authority to move off in a different direction and had no duty to ask a court to look into decisions Maria had made as trustee. Ms. Ramirez said she would check to be sure there were no conflicts of interest to worry about and, if there were none, she would be pleased to serve as our expert

witness -- at $500 an hour. Since this seemed to be the
going rate these days for expert witnesses, and since it was
my hope that, when the case was finally over, Duane
Thurston would be ordered to reimburse Scott for any expert
witness fee he incurred, I told Ms. Ramirez her proposed fee
was acceptable.

We also discussed the issue that comes up when
expert witnesses express opinions about issues of law, which
she would need to do in this case. The problem here comes
from the fact that trial court judges decide issues of law and,
since they are supposed to know the law themselves, they
don't need, and shouldn't allow, an expert witness to tell
them how to do their job. In that regard, some judges
nonetheless appreciate help from an expert witness. Others,
however, prohibit testimony from an expert witness on a
technical issue of law. Ms. Ramirez did not know Judge
Elefson and had no idea which side of this log he might fall
off on. She said, however, that in her prior engagements as
an expert witness this had not become a problem. She was
able to present her opinion testimony in a way that did an
end run around the issue and did not appear as a lecture on
the law to a judge who, in theory, already knew the law.

We ended our phone call with an agreement that Ms.
Ramirez would complete her conflicts check and, if there
were none, she would send me an engagement letter
confirming her status as an expert witness for Scott. I
received the engagement letter two days later and promptly
filed an expert witness endorsement with the court. Manifort
would now dredge up a counter expert who would challenge
Regina Ramirez' opinions and testify that Scott, while he
was representing Maria as the trustee of the Thurston Family
Trust, had duties running directly to the trust's beneficiaries,

meaning Duane and Billie, and Phillip. This witness would testify that, in his or her opinion, Scott had a duty to inform Maria that she had to tell the beneficiaries she was changing the terms of the trust agreement dealing with their distributions and, if she didn't do that, he, Scott, would have to tell them. This witness would also presumably testify that, once Scott became trustee, he had a duty, on behalf of the beneficiaries, to ask a probate court to rule whether Maria, as successor trustee to Andy, in fact had authority to rewrite the trust agreement and reduce the distributions coming to Duane and Billie that Andy Thurston had originally put in the trust agreement. I was sure Manifort would have no problem -- at probably $700 an hour -- finding someone who would serve as a counter expert on Duane's behalf and issue these opinions in support of Duane's claims in the case.

I promptly signed and returned Ms. Ramirez' engagement letter. I also sent her several documents intended to help her ramp up on the case. This included a copy of Scott Freeman's impressive resume; the trust agreement for the Thurston Family Trust as originally written and the amendment that Maria had made reducing the distributions to Duane and Billie; the complaint and answer/counterclaim filed in the lawsuit; the transcripts of the depositions of Duane Thurston and Scott; my motion asking the judge to rule on an issue of law; and Manifort's response to that motion. Because an expert witness's file is subject to discovery and is not protected by the attorney-client privilege, I did not, much as I wanted to, include any commentary from me to Ms. Ramirez to the effect that this lawsuit against Scott was an act of extortion on Duane's part since, after Maria's death, he couldn't figure out anyone else to sue.

Next up on my to-do list was the matter of choosing a mediator. This had to be done since Judge Elefson had ordered the parties to engage in mediation in pursuit of a settlement and would not allow the case to proceed to trial until mediation had occurred. The names Manifort had given me as mediators acceptable to him were all experienced and well-respected retired judges. But, one stood out to me as being better qualified for this case than the others -- Homer Weatherspoon. Weatherspoon had spent twenty-five years in private practice with a medium size Austin law firm practicing trusts and estates law and then twenty-five years as a probate court judge. He graduated from the same law school I did -- the University of California at Berkley -- and, most importantly, his online bio said he was a fly fisherman.

I told Manifort in an email that Weatherspoon was my choice from his list and that he should go ahead and engage him as our mediator and get some available dates from him for a half day mediation. The plan was for Scott and me to appear virtually. Manifort and Duane could appear in person if they so chose. I remained firmly of the belief that mediation was not going to resolve this lawsuit since any settlement would require Scott to contradict Maria's decisions about distribution of the assets of the Thurston Family Trust and he was never going to do that. Scott knew what Maria wanted, and why, and she was now dead and his job was to carry out her decisions. He would not violate the confidence she had placed in him, notwithstanding that his personal assets had now been put at risk by Duane Thurston's lawsuit.

At the end of the day, I went back to the hospital to see how Scott was doing. He was sitting up in bed with a laptop and a cell phone, trying to answer emails and give instructions to his staff and the other lawyers at his firm who had thrown themselves into some of his projects. The hospital was no longer allowing Scott to drip narcotic pain medicine into his body and he was totally coherent, but tired.

"Hello McConnell. They're telling me I can go home tomorrow. Apparently my complaining about the lime Jell-O and the noise in this place, and the absence of any baseball games on the television service they subscribe to, has won out over their desire to keep me around as a revenue enhancing opportunity."

"So how are you feeling?"

"Like someone who just had his chest slit open and various body parts molested. But I can deal with all of that at home as well as here. Stella will do just fine as a rehabilitation supervisor and she will never, I don't believe, try to feed me lime Jell-O."

I then gave Scott a rundown on my expert witness and mediator decisions, and I told him I had nothing yet to report about the defamatory social media attack on his son Jeff or Ed's (and Veronica's) efforts to track down Duane Thurston's possible involvement in the illegal street marketing of prescription pain meds. And I had heard nothing further from Attorney Regulation Counsel about the grievance Duane Thurston had filed accusing Scott of violating the Colorado Rules of Professional Conduct.

As I was getting ready to leave, Scott held out his hand to me and I grasped it. It was limp but warm. "Jack, thank you for being my lawyer and, more importantly, for being my friend. True friends are hard to find these days. I appreciate everything you have done for me."

I nodded, let go of his hand with tears in my eyes and headed home to give Elsie a short walk around my neighborhood and an on-time dinner.

After Elsie had her dinner and I consumed a glass of chardonnay and a left-over piece of chicken thrown into a salad, I put in a call to Veronica.

"Hello Jack. How are things on the southern front?"

"OK, I guess. We spread RJ's ashes, and Abby's ashes, at the place RJ had selected. Scott is due to be released from the hospital tomorrow and begin what will be a lengthy rehab at home, with Stella in charge. I found a good expert witness for the Texas lawsuit and agreed on a mediator I thought was appropriate for this litigation. Things are crazy busy in my office but that's probably good. Otherwise, I'd have too much time to be unhappy about the ways of the world and what's been happening to Scott and how work is getting in the way of fishing."

"Well, I can report that I've been in touch with Ed, not during Fed work time and not handing out government secrets. But, I was able to offer him a few suggestions about how to he might be able to find who perpetrated the internet attack on Scott's son and what Duane Thurston might have been up to in regard to the illicit sale of prescription pain meds."

"Thanks Veronica, on both fronts. One way or another, I need to get Scott out from under the legal chaos his efforts at being a good lawyer have brought to him. When are you coming down to Colorado Springs to see Elsie and me? Jupiter and Venus will both be shining brightly on my deck this weekend, and I bought some new furniture I thought we should try."

Chapter 24

On Thursday, I received Judge Elefson's decision on my motion asking him to rule on an issue of law. Not surprisingly, he denied the motion, with the usual excuse judges use -- that there were unresolved issues of fact running around somewhere in the case and, until those issues were decided by a jury, he could not rule on issues of law. His order read as follows:

> "Defendant Freeman has filed a motion asking the court to rule on an issue of law concerning the duty of a lawyer representing a trustee of a trust, and who later became the successor trustee of the trust, to take certain actions, and provide certain information, affecting the beneficiaries of the trust. The court concludes that the questions presented by defendant Freeman involve mixed issues of fact and law and therefore the court cannot answer a question of law until the questions of fact in the case have been established by the jury. Defendant's motion is therefore denied, without prejudice. The court will deal with issues of law after the facts of the case have been established."

I thought about filing another motion asking Elefson to reconsider his decision because, as I had already told him in my original motion, he could assume all facts in the case were exactly as the plaintiffs said they were, and therefore there were no issues of fact to get in his way. But, I'd been in this situation enough times before to know a motion to reconsider would be denied, and would merely irritate the judge. So, my strategy for getting the judge to issue an order saying my view of the law governing this case was correct, and that Scott Freeman didn't owe duties to Duane and Billie as beneficiaries of the Thurston Family Trust while Maria was the trustee, was a dead end. Nonetheless, my motion at least had the benefit of getting the judge thinking about the unusual legal issues this case presented and hopefully teeing things up for a decision in my favor down the road a bit.

On Friday, I checked in with Scott by phone and confirmed that he had indeed been released from the hospital and was home, on a short rehabilitation leash controlled by Stella. I told him about Judge Elefson's order denying my motion to rule on an issue of law and told him I had decided to go fishing for the rest of the day since other matters in my office seemed to be in a holding pattern -- for better or for worse. Although Scott, after his cardiovascular accident, was more receptive than he used to be to the idea that lawyers needed to occasionally engage in stress relieving activities, he nonetheless couldn't resist saying: "Fine, McConnell, abandon your client at a time of great need and go fishing. I'll get over it."

Today's fishing venue was a stretch of the Middle Fork of the South Platte River just upstream from Spinney Mountain Reservoir. Sometimes, the rainbow trout, which spawn in the spring, move up into the river from the reservoir in pursuit of fish sex. My hope was that this activity would still be going on and that the high runoff from snow melt, which would make the river unfishable, was not yet underway.

As always, the drive up Ute Pass and into the mountains was a relaxing experience and crossing over Wilkerson Summit gave me a majestic view of the Mosquito Range to the west, the Park Range to the north, and the Sangre de Cristo mountains to the south. Immediately before me was South Park, a high mountain desert famous for wind, snow drifts, pronghorn antelope and law enforcement since, if there was ever a place that invited speeding, this was it.

I was probably a week late in chasing the rainbows coming out of Spinney Mountain Reservoir and up into the South Platte River ("you should have been here last week...") but I was able to tie into two nice hook-jawed males who gave me a good battle before I could bring them to net and release them back into the river. My Adams 12 flies were of no use. The fish I caught went after streamers -- flies imitating little fish that get eaten by bigger fish. The feeding activity shut down around 4 p.m. and I packed up and headed home, a 90-minute drive. On the way home, I listened to Dvorak's New World Symphony on the CD player in my aging SUV, a piece of music that always had a stress relieving benefit. New cars don't even have CD players. All the more reason to keep what I already have.

When I made it home, Veronica's Subaru (again seriously in need of a wash) was in the driveway and she, glass of chardonnay in hand, and Elsie, chew toy by her side, were on the deck enjoying the late afternoon warmth of a spring day. Veronica gave me a nice hug and a kiss and Elsie gave me an acceptable tail wag. I poured myself a glass of wine and joined them on the deck.

"Hi Veronica. You look great as always, but tired."

"It's been a long week, where Fed politics were regularly getting in the way of my doing my job. But mid-week my team of computer jocks was able to nab a cohort of people trying to feed misinformation into the internet and trying to orchestrate a possibly violent protest in front of the Boston Federal Reserve Bank at the end of next week. They're now out of business and a couple of them have been arrested. But this is all pretty scary. We used to devote our energies to shutting down external terrorist threats. Now, we're more concerned with domestic terrorists who seem to be intent on ripping the country apart, for who knows what purpose. I suppose for some people it's just frustration that their plight in life isn't what they were promised and doesn't seem to be getting any better."

I brought Veronica up to speed on Scott's medical and legal situation and asked if she'd had further dialogue with Ed.

"Well, as you know, I have to be careful here since I can't share with him -- or you -- surveillance technology developed by the government, but I did give Ed a couple of suggestions about how he might monitor internet chatter concerning the derogatory information about Jeff Freeman. This might help him track down whoever was behind the sexual misconduct post that got him -- guilty until proven innocent -- in trouble. I also shared with Ed some thoughts about illicit drug activity Duane Thurston might be involved in. It's largely public information these days that organized crime has latched onto the market for prescription pain meds, resulting from addictions to these drugs. Doctors can't prescribe the meds anymore without getting in trouble and worse from their point of view, they can't bill Medicare and Medicaid, or private health insurance plans, for their services trying to help people wean themselves off these drugs. So, people with this powerful addiction are left to try to find the drugs they are craving on the street -- and there's big money being generated by illicit traffic in these drugs."

"Not to change the subject or anything, but I bought some fresh-made crab cakes from our last remaining fish store in Colorado Springs, Fish Tales, for dinner. So I'm going to get started on that. And then, after dinner, I thought we could sit out on the back deck and watch the dark sky roll in. This is a new moon night, so the brightest objects in the sky will be Jupiter and Saturn."

"Were you also thinking about your new deck furniture by any chance?"

"Possibly."

"I thought the old furniture worked just fine the last time I was down here. But OK, you work on the crab cakes. And feed this poor dog her dinner so she won't act like she's being abused. I'm going to take a shower and try out the new spray-on bottle of Shalimar I just bought at an outrageous price."

Dinner turned out great, since all you do with pre-made crab cakes is heat them up. I also put together a simple salad of tomatoes, avocados, Monterey jack cheese, dried cherries and walnuts, and I took out of the freezer and heated a loaf of French bread from Le Bistro Saint Tropez I'd been saving for such an occasion. Dessert was a piece of Ghiradelli chocolate and a glass of Port wine for each of us, and a test drive of the new deck furniture. Spray-on Shalimar, I decided, was a nice enhancement for the product. I thought perhaps I should do an internet endorsement but, for a variety of reasons, decided against it.

Chapter 25

Veronica had to head back to Denver late Saturday morning, so I spent a little time in the office catching up on my work and then Elsie and I made a hike in Bear Creek Park. She had to be on a leash here but she didn't seem to mind. We passed other mostly well-behaved dogs who wanted to share a nose rub and a butt sniff with Elsie, which she seemed to enjoy, or at least tolerate. There was, however, one Rottweiler who charged at us and had to be dragged off the trail by its embarrassed and apologetic owner. Elsie was less focused than Fletcher had been on claiming territory along this route so we made better time than I did with Fletcher.

Sunday was another catch up day in the office where, as usual, the absence of distractions from phone calls and emails made doing work on motions, briefs, trial preparation and the like easier, and sometimes even enjoyable.

The following Wednesday, I headed up to Denver to, at her request, have an informal meeting with Jocelyn Alvarez, Attorney Regulation Counsel, to discuss the grievance Duane Thurston had filed against Scott claiming he had breached ethical duties owing to Duane and Billie as beneficiaries of the Thurston Family Trust. Ms. Alvarez had a modest office in the Ralph L. Carr Colorado Judicial Center, where the Colorado Supreme Court and the Colorado Court of Appeals conduct their business. Ralph Carr had left his mark on the history of Colorado when, as governor, he opposed (unsuccessfully) the incarceration of people of Japanese descent following the attack on Pearl Harbor.

Although this was the right thing to do, it was widely unpopular and ended his political career.

As usual, finding a place to park in downtown Denver that didn't risk damage to my SUV and didn't involve confiscatory charges was a problem, but I finally found a spot in an open-air parking lot a mere four blocks from the Carr building that was acceptable and allowed me to show up on time for my 2:00 p.m. appointment with Jocelyn Alvarez.

Ms. Alvarez met me after a short wait in the lobby area of her office and ushered me into a modestly furnished (government standard) conference room. She was short -- maybe five foot two -- a bit on the plumb side, fifty-something years old and with greying mid-length hair. I know I'm not supposed to have this kind of thought but, well, frumpy came to mind as way to describe her. As a redeeming attribute, Ms. Alvarez was articulate and had a charming soft southern accent, from North Carolina she told me, where she grew up.

Ms. Alvarez: "Mr. McConnell, thanks for coming to Denver for this meeting. I suppose we could have done this on the phone, or by Zoom, but I'm still a face-to-face-meeting kind of lawyer."

Me: "I concur. A virtual get-together just doesn't lend itself to a fully candid exchange of ideas."

Ms. Alvarez: "To cut to the chase, this grievance has generated a fair amount of controversy in my office. As you know, we only look at ethical violations, not civil claims for damages. But, sometimes they overlap. In any event, the grievance filer, Duane Thurston, has pitched us on the proposition that your client, Scott Freeman, owed duties to him and his brother William -- who is apparently intellectually challenged -- because they were beneficiaries of a trust and your client was the lawyer for the trustee, and the trustee amended the trust agreement to greatly reduce their right to a distribution from the trust. And your client didn't take any action to inform Duane and William that their interests in the trust were being impaired. By the time they found out about the amendment, Duane Thurston says, their ability to challenge it was eliminated by the death of the trustee."

Me: "For purposes of this meeting, let's say that's all correct. But we stridently dispute the proposition that the lawyer for a trustee of a trust is therefore a lawyer for the beneficiaries of the trust or is somehow responsible for duties the trustee might have to beneficiaries of the trust. The lawyer for the trustee should be able to provide legal advice to the trustee without being subject to ambush by beneficiaries."

Ms. Alvarez: "We understand your argument but, as you know, the Rules of Professional Conduct now include the idea that lawyers, in some circumstances, owe duties to third parties who are not their clients. So, even if we reject Duane Thurston's argument that your client somehow became his lawyer, we still have this problem that lawyers owe duties to parties who are not their client. Maybe you can chalk this up to politics, but the Supreme Court has told my office to push hard on the idea that lawyers owe duties to non-client third parties. In any event, here's what we can offer Scott Freeman -- a private letter of reprimand. This will not be published in any way and will not be available to the press or the public. Its only real significance is that, if he becomes a frequent flier in my office because of additional grievances, this will be strike one and he'll be at risk of more stringent sanctions for those subsequent claims."

Me: "Ms. Alvarez, I'll certainly present your offer to Scott, but I can tell you right now he won't accept it. He is firmly of the belief that he has violated no ethical duty to anyone and, instead, he has fully met his duties owing to his client, Maria Thurston, who is now dead. He is being sued in Texas by Duane Thurston, with his brother William -- Billie -- being dragged along, and that lawsuit, together with this grievance, is an attempt at extortion. Scott, in his current capacity as the successor trustee to the Thurston Family Trust, cannot, and will not, authorize the trust to make distributions to Duane and Billie that Maria Thurston, as the successor trustee to her husband, Andrew, following his death, did not authorize. Among other reasons, Scott couldn't do this because it would appear to be an act intended to protect his personal assets from attack by Duane Thurston. As the successor trustee for the Thurston Family Trust, after Maria's death, he can't be shoveling out assets of the trust to protect his own assets. And he's not about to reach into his own pocket to settle a claim he believes is frivolous and groundless. Basically, we think this grievance needs to be dismissed and, if that's not going to happen, then we need to tee it up for a hearing, and after that however many appeals it takes to get to the root of the issue here. But, I'll do my duty and tell Scott what you have offered. At the moment, he's home recovering from open-heart surgery and this may have some effect on how he looks at this situation. His primary care doctor, and longtime friend, has told him he needs to shed stress in his life and your offer would give him an opportunity to do that."

We ended our meeting with Jocelyn Alvarez, at my request, giving me a tour of the Ralph L. Carr Colorado Judicial Center. Since I had not had any recent cases before the Colorado Court of Appeals or Supreme Court, this was my first visit to this relatively new building and I wanted to see what upgrades had been made to the court rooms where those courts hold oral arguments. The court rooms were nice -- attractive, functional and not so ostentatious as to offend taxpayers. It was nonetheless my hope that the grievance against Scott Freeman didn't end up here.

Since the Judicial Center was right next door to the Denver Art Museum, and my meeting with Jocelyn Alvarez had not taken as long as I had anticipated, I spent a pleasant forty-five minutes at the museum viewing a traveling surrealist exhibit the museum had brought to Denver. I became a fan of surrealism many years ago when, on a rare business trip to Paris, I had a chance to visit the Museum of Modern Art. Paintings that took real things and spun them into imaginary objects or inserted them into out of place environments struck a chord with me, although I don't know why. I actually now own a signed lithograph by one of the famous European surrealists, Max Ernst, as a gift from Veronica. It hangs in my living room (next to a large plastic model of a rainbow trout I purchased at a Trout Unlimited fund raiser).

I made it out of Denver -- with no damage to my SUV from parking lot close encounters -- before afternoon grid lock set in on I-25 and listened to a Rockies game on the radio on my way back to Colorado Springs. The Rockies were actually ahead and the bullpen was holding the fort. I bailed on going back to my office and instead went home to give Elsie a walk up into Section 16, a beautiful open space area on the west side of town. This was a pleasant diversion for both of us -- until we encountered a group of coyotes who were trying to lure Elsie into a friendly little romp in pursuit of then attacking her and turning her into a meal. We retreated to the safety of my front porch, with a bone from the grocery store for Elsie and a glass of wine for me.

Thursday morning, I stopped by Scott's home to tell him about my meeting with Ms. Alvarez. Scott was at his kitchen table, with a laptop, telephone and several client files in front of him. He was wearing what I would consider upscale gym attire, which I'm sure Stella had purchased for him in an effort to make him modestly more presentable during his at-home convalescence.

"Hello McConnell. Thanks for stopping by. How did your meeting go with the Attorney Regulation Counsel?"

I told Scott about the meeting and the offer of settlement being made to him involving a private letter of reprimand.

"No way in hell, Jack. I did not violate any ethical duties owing to anyone. As I've told you a dozen times, I would have violated an ethical duty if I had disclosed Maria's attorney-client confidential information to Duane Thurston. The whole idea behind the attorney-client privilege is to create a circumstance where a client can trust and confide in his or her lawyer. As a lawyer, I have a duty to protect and preserve confidential information received from a client. If I had told Duane that Maria was amending the trust agreement -- because she thought he was a snake -- I would have violated that duty. Doesn't anybody get this other than me and, hopefully, you?"

"Well, when, in a moment of weakness I may still learn to regret, I agreed to be your lawyer, I considered my job in large part to be to disentangle you from legal controversy in pursuit of reducing stress in your life. So here's a chance to do that. The letter of reprimand will be private. It won't be anything Duane can use in the Texas lawsuit. It will go into some electronic file never to be seen again. This would be like getting a traffic citation for not coming to a complete stop at a stop sign and settling the matter, as the Colorado Springs city attorney's office is known to do, by agreeing to plead guilty to a burned-out taillight."

"No. The answer is no. I will not plead guilty to an ethical violation that didn't happen just to be done with the matter. You can tell Ms. Alvarez I appreciate her efforts but she can go to hell."

"I don't think I'll quite say it that way, but I will tell her the offer she has made is rejected and she'll need to move this grievance along to the next level, whatever that is. I think the next level is a hearing of some sort but I'm not positive of that. This is a new playing field for me and I'm not quite sure how they do things. But, that issue having been decided, how are you doing on the recovery front"

"OK, I guess. I'm still sore as heck where they busted through my chest to get to my heart valves, and sometimes my heart goes into a kind of fluttering mode which is a little unsettling. But Rollie stopped by yesterday and said I was right on track for a full recovery and I should get my butt out of this chair and start moving around more. He also went into great detail about his colonoscopy, which I could have done without."

"I'll inform Ms. Alvarez of your decision on her offer. The next thing you and I need to do is prepare for our mediation with our Texas mediator, Homer Weatherspoon.

That's coming up in two weeks. I'm working on a mediation statement to send to him in advance of the mediation. I'll run that by you before I send it to Weatherspoon but I don't think you'll have to spend much time on it. The mediation statement will recite the facts involved in Maria's decision to reduce the distributions to Duane and Billie, your activities as Maria's lawyer, and your current status as successor trustee for the Thurston Family Trust. We'll tell the mediator you have no interest in a settlement, which would need to involve either assets of the trust or your personal assets being paid to Duane and Billie. I'll tell him the only settlement acceptable to you is a dismissal of the lawsuit, including dismissal of the counterclaim you filed against Duane for abuse of process and malicious prosecution. In other words, a mutual dismissal of claims."

"You got it. Jack, thanks again for being my lawyer -- and my friend."

Chapter 26

On Friday, Ed checked in. He was in his bus and back at his favorite RV campground north of San Francisco, just up the road from Stinson Beach, with an awesome view of the Pacific Ocean.

"Hi Jack. A beautiful day in these parts, although the drought is really taking its toll on Northern California and this entire area looks like it could be the venue for the next wildfire, in which event I would have trouble getting out of here. Well, listen, I think we've had a breakthrough in connection with the Jeff Freeman defamation situation. And, I don't think Duane Thurston was the source of the internet post that got him in trouble. I think the malicious actor here may be a member or former member of one of the volleyball teams Jeff Freeman has coached."

"Wow. Tell me more."

"As I indicated earlier, I had decided I wanted to tune in a bit to teenage gossip concerning the allegations against Jeff. And in that regard, I've been assisted by a startup technology company called Forensic Filtering, Inc. -- FFI. You may recall that FFI helped us in the counterfeit cashier's check case, where we were able to identify one of the bad guys using a voice recognition system FFI had developed. FFI has now been around two-plus years and is doing a brisk business selling data search and internet surveillance technology to private companies and to federal, state and local government agencies, including all of the U.S. military branches. You may also recall that the two guys who started this company, who met while they were classmates at MIT, needed to learn more about how to think like a private investigator, so I tutored them on that. As a thank you, they occasionally let me use some of their tools. One of those tools allows for a real time monitoring of internet social media platforms and text messaging traffic, searching for names and other information the system is told to look for. So, FFI and I put together a monitoring protocol with the key words being Jeff Freeman and various of the terms used in the anonymous internet post that accused him of sexual misconduct. What we captured with this system were lots of emails and text messages among and between students at Jeff's high school. And one player on this stage kept showing up repeatedly, either as a party to an email or a text message, or a person being talked about – gossiped about -- by others. Her name is Priscilla Dalton and I think she may be the author of the defamatory post about Jeff. But there are still some questions that need to be answered before we land firmly on that square. Would you be willing to call Jeff and see what he can tell you about Priscilla Dalton?"

"Yes, I can do that, and thanks Ed. That's great work. I assume there's a home run hour in here somewhere."

"Too early to tell."

"In any event, I assume what you and FFI have been doing is legal, right?"

"Let's save that discussion for another day."

"I thought you might say that. So, what about Duane Thurston's drug trafficking activity? Any news there?"

"No. We're going to have to go boots on the ground for that and see if we can find someone who is willing to talk about how prescription narcotic pain medicine is finding its way onto the street. And, I may need you and Veronica to help with that. But, I warn you in advance we're going to be dealing with a tightly organized criminal enterprise which has been known to protect against information leaks with all means available, including an occasional mysterious disappearance."

"Swell. Well, at least thanks for the heads up."

"Jack, you and Veronica did great as clandestine agents and spies in the counterfeit cashier's check case. I'm sure you'll do just fine here as well."

"Yeah, but I don't think you told us in the cashier's check case that people might be wanting to kill us."

"That was an oversight. I probably should have. Apologies."

"I'll let you know what Jeff Freeman has to say about Priscilla Dalton. And please let me know what you have in mind with regard to Duane Thurston that's going to require us to stick our necks out. I may want to talk to a life insurance agent before we go down that path."

After my call with Ed, I put in a call to Scott and briefed him on what Ed had told me, leaving out, however, the part about boots on the ground and mysterious disappearances.

"That certainly is a surprise, and a change of direction, about Jeff. Let me know what Jeff can tell you about this Priscilla Dalton."

"Will do."

In further neglect of legal work I should have been doing, I called Jeff Freeman, who was out planting zucchini in his garden.

"Hi Jeff. Sorry to interrupt your agricultural pursuits, but do you have a few minutes to talk with me about the defamation incident?"

"Of course. Have we learned anything about where the internet post that got me in trouble came from?"

"Maybe." I then told him some of what Ed had come up with and asked him to tell me about Priscilla Dalton.

"What does she have to do with this?"

"We think she might have had some involvement in the internet post accusing you of misconduct."

"Wow. That's certainly surprising news. But here's what I can tell you. Priscilla is now a senior, due to graduate in a few weeks. She was on the school volleyball team her sophomore and junior years, and at the start of her senior year. She was a so-so player and not a starter, but she trained hard and was an asset to the team, and she got a fair amount of playing time. But, she was removed from the team because her grades suddenly went south and that disqualified her. Part of the problem there was that I gave her a failing grade in an analytical geometry course last semester. She largely blew off the course -- didn't always do homework, sometimes didn't show up for class, missed a couple of tests that were part of the course. I gave her fair warning that a failing grade was coming and offered to tutor her, but none of that worked to get her back on track. And, after the failing grade, school policy required her removal from the team."

"What about her personal life?"

"I don't think she has a lot of friends. She's a loner. And I think she has a tough situation at home. Her parents are divorced and she's in a shared custody situation, with her parents either not wanting anything to do with her or competing with each other to win her affections. And her only sibling -- an older brother -- is in a juvenile detention center in Buena Vista because of an armed robbery conviction."

"Other than for your analytical geometry course, has she been an OK student?"

"Yes, and perhaps of note here, she is a technology whiz kid. I also teach a computer literacy course and she was way ahead of everyone else -- and frankly way ahead of me -- in that course. She started coding when she was ten and, right now, could move into a high-level position at just about any technology company on the planet."

"Do you think she was angry about getting a failing grade from you and being booted off the volleyball team?"

"I don't really know that. Could be. Like I said, she's a very private kid and this is certainly nothing we ever talked about. But, in thinking about it now, I believe she has been carrying around a big burden of anger about, probably, lots of things. It's hard being an adolescent girl these days in the best of circumstances, and life hasn't given her the best of circumstances. In any event, I suppose I could have been on her evil teacher list because of that failing grade and her removal from the team."

"Thanks Jeff. That's enough for now. If it turns out Priscilla Dalton in fact had some involvement in the internet post that got you in trouble, there will be lots of issues to deal with concerning consequences. You might as well start thinking about that while you're planting your garden. Civil damages? Criminal prosecution? Denial of right to graduate?"

After my conversation with Jeff, I cycled back to Ed and Scott and told them what Jeff had told me.

"Jack," Ed said, "I have some addition information that points at Priscilla Dalton. Again with help from my friends at Forensic Filtering, I was able to work back through several of the layers of encryption that went into the InstaFlip post slamming Jeff and I found, through a dark web company that sells internet defamation services, footprints identifying a tablet computer that that ties to Priscilla Dalton. So, I think she's our culprit in the Jeff Freeman defamation event. The question now becomes -- what do with do with this information?"

"Let me suggest this as a game plan. I'll go back to Charlie Justin, the lawyer from the Colorado Educators Association who is representing Jeff, tell him what we know, and ask him to present this information to the lawyer representing the school district, with a request that the school district then confront Priscilla Dalton with our suspicions and see what she says. If she confesses to being the author of, or otherwise involved in, the defamation, we can get Jeff reinstated to his teaching position immediately, get an apology from the school district for the trouble it's caused, and get Charlie's attorney's fees covered. And then Jeff and the school district will have to decide what punishments might be imposed on this kid."

"I agree. Our evidence here is skimpy at best, but my bet is that Priscilla Dalton, when confronted in this manner, will admit to her sins, especially if she understands a denial could result in far more serious sanctions, including a criminal prosecution."

Chapter 27

Over the weekend, on Saturday, I took Cooper on another fly fishing adventure, this time to a small stretch of the Middle Fork of the South Platte River that runs through Tomahawk State Wildlife Area, west of Colorado Springs between Hartsel and Fairplay. Most of the fish in the river here are small but an occasional lunker can be tricked out from under the shelter of a cut-away bank. Cooper's fly casting had improved considerably with his front yard practice (mostly intended to impress Amy) and his first efforts at tying his own flies had produced some respectable Hare's Ears, so those were the flies we used on this trip. Over the course of two hours of fishing, we each caught two small brown trout which were immediately returned to the river, and Cooper was pumped up at catching his first fish on a fly he had tied himself. All in all, a good trip.

On the way home, a 75-minute drive, we had a chance to talk about Cooper's thought that maybe he wanted to go to law school and become a lawyer, inspired, apparently, by me. I told him again that I went to law school to stall on making important life decisions, had no intention of actually becoming a lawyer, and ended up having a love/hate relationship with the practice of law, as it had been dished up to me. My slice of the legal profession, I told him, had, for many years while I was working at a large big city firm, mostly involved helping rich people exchange money in various ways, either by buying and selling things or fighting over having tried. I told him, however, that having a legal education offered benefits outside the practice of law and I certainly didn't want to talk him out of going to law school as a next step on his life's journey. I just wanted him to think more about what was important to him and what he felt his personal talents were, and to look for a match. (I also reminded myself that I should engage in this same analysis but never seemed to do so.)

On Monday, I had a lengthy phone conversation with Charlie Justin. He concurred with the game plan Ed and I had discussed and said he would put the plan in play. He called me back on Thursday and told me the confrontation with Priscilla Dalton had occurred the previous day, with Priscilla's mother, but not her father, present. Priscilla broke down and confessed that she had authored and, through a dark web seller of defamation services, coordinated the delivery of the InstaFlip post accusing Jeff Freeman of inappropriate sexual conduct to the parents of volleyball team members, past and present, and select members of the school district administration. She said she was in fact angry at Jeff for the failing grade he gave her in analytical geometry, was angry at Jeff for not giving her more playing time on the volleyball team, was angry at the school district for having rules that forced her to be removed from the team, and was angry at life in general for a long list of things. The meeting ended with the school district's attorney, Louisa Gardner, telling Priscilla and her mother that the board of education would decide what sanctions would be imposed, including a possible referral of the matter to the district attorney's office and a possible cancellation of her right to graduate with her class. Charlie told her he didn't know if Jeff Freeman would pursue a civil lawsuit against her for defamation. Both Ms. Gardner and Charlie told Priscilla and her mother that it might be a good idea for Priscilla to have a lawyer.

After Priscilla, still sobbing, and her mother left the room, Charlie and Louisa Gardner had a brief conversation wherein Charlie was assured that Jeff would immediately be reinstated as a teacher at his school and all compensation and benefits would be fully restored. Charlie told her this likely wouldn't be enough and that the school district's knee jerk, guilty-until-proven-innocent, handling of this matter might be the source of a claim by Jeff for damages. Charlie then gave Jeff a call and brought him up to speed on these events.

I also put in calls to Jeff and his father, and we agreed that, the next afternoon, we would get together and talk about what happens next. Jeff said he would drive down to Colorado Springs, so we could have a face-to-face meeting. Jeff had only seen Scott once since the bypass surgery, making this a good time for a visit with his father in any event.

Jeff was a handsome, fit and articulate thirty-five-year-old, and was someone I immediately liked. Scott declined the opportunity to be an "I'll call the shots here, dude" kind of father and brought his gifts for rational thought and patience to the meeting. Our first topic of conversation was Scott's recovery from his surgery. He was doing OK, he told us. At Rollie Dumbarton's insistence, he was walking at least two miles every day and Stella, still in full control of a short rehabilitation leash, saw to it that no alcoholic beverages were consumed.

I told Jeff there were certainly grounds here for a civil lawsuit for damages, both against the school district and Priscilla, although how those damages would be measured was problematic. We were into the blurry world of emotional distress and reputation injury damages, which could be whatever a jury decided they should be. I also told

Jeff a criminal prosecution was possible. At age 18, Priscilla could be tried as an adult for various high tech, internet related crimes. It's unlikely she would receive a prison sentence, but an attention-getting fine and a lengthy probation with numerous activity restrictions would seem likely. Of greater consequence, perhaps, is that she would then enter adult life with an options-limiting criminal record that would follow her around for the rest of her days. Finally, I told Jeff that getting the damaging post taken down and no longer picked up by search engines like Google was a priority but could be challenging.

"I've given all of this lots of thought," Jeff finally said. "Priscilla Dalton is a talented, troubled adolescent who has had to walk through a mine field of life's dirty tricks just to stay in school, avoid getting tied up with drugs, and deal with a painful parental split. I want her to learn from this experience but nothing more. I want her to stay in school and graduate with her class. I want her to cooperate in investigating the company she found that sells internet defamation services and in developing a strategy to take down the InstaFlip post and stop its spread. I want her to have a chance to go to college and nurture her talents as a technology prodigy. I want her to know I don't condone what she did, which was off-the-charts wrong, but I forgive her for what she did. Jack, my dad can tell you a few things I did as an adolescent that fell well below his threshold of acceptable behavior and might have scarred me with a criminal record if it hadn't been for his patience and thoughtful counsel. We worked through all that and I learned the value of forgiveness, although my allowance took a serious hit, as did my driving privileges."

Me: "Do you want to pursue any kind of claim against the school district, which never should have taken you out of the classroom without an investigation and without due process -- a right to defend against the charges being thrown at you?"

"No. I would like an apology from the district and an agreement that Priscilla can move on to graduation without some kind of disciplinary action showing up on her transcript. And I would like the district, as a punishment of sorts for Priscilla, to require her to tutor any kid in the district who's interested in learning computer coding. And the school district needs to pay Charlie Justin's attorney's fees. Paying money to the teacher's union will be a meaningful punishment for the district since it considers the union -- the Colorado Educators Association -- to be public enemy number one. Finally, the school district needs to take whatever action is required, and pay whatever costs are involved, to get the InstaFlip post taken down and stop it from being picked up by internet searches for Jeff Freeman. And InstaFlip needs to post a notice on its site stating its earlier post about me was a fabrication and wholly false. All of that might be a hard sell to the school board whose members are likely to get beaten up by staff, teachers, parents, students and media outlets looking for a nice juicy scandal to help increase advertising revenue. But maybe they'll see the wisdom in keeping all of this as quiet as possible, especially since several of them are coming up for election in the fall."

Me: "We'll do our best to pursue that plan. Since getting sued and slammed with embarrassing publicity is the school district's other alternative, it should find your proposal quite acceptable. And the district has people in its public relations department trained and experienced in scandal management and a technology staff that can take on the task of removing the defamatory material from the internet and otherwise procuring cooperation from InstaFlip through appropriate threats of legal action."

Scott: "Son, I've never been more proud of you. And yes, I did forgive you for stealing our neighbor's car and going for a joy ride when you were 16."

Jeff: "Thanks to both of you. Let me know how this plays out. In the meantime, I have to get back home and work on lesson plans, and find out what's left of the volleyball team."

With that, Jeff gave his father a soft hug (appropriate for someone who just had open heart surgery) and headed out the door.

"Thanks Jack. I guess my request that you be my lawyer had a few more moving parts than I anticipated. You can always quit, of course."

"Not yet, but that's good to know. What really scares me about Jeff's experience is how easy it is to destroy someone's life using social media and the internet, and that companies are out there selling character destroying services and then trying to extract ransoms to remove their posts. And it saddens me how quickly people are willing to ignore truth and jump at the chance to find pleasure from someone else's pain."

Before leaving, I asked Scott how things were going with Phillip.

"We're on our game plan there. We have agreed on a budget and he is sticking to it. His children are behaving responsibly. He has told me he currently has no interest in trying to rehabilitate a relationship with Duane, although he does have such an interest with Billie. Speaking of Billie, he seems to be oblivious to what Duane is up to and has no thoughts about what Maria did to reduce his take from the Thurston Family Trust. The trust is continuing to pay his rent and other living expenses, and I have found an art gallery in town interested in showing his paintings. At some point, I need to decide if I should have a guardian and conservator appointed to keep him safe and manage his money. For the moment, I'm taking on those duties myself as successor trustee of the Thurston Family Trust and that's working OK. But, for his sake and mine, I don't want that to go on forever. Since Duane has seen fit to drag him along in the Texas lawsuit, there's not much more I can do until that matter reaches an end, whatever it turns out to be. So, bottom line, Phillip's and Billie's situations appear to be under control."

After my meeting with Jeff and Scott, I headed to the Y for a three-mile jog (well, maybe a two-mile jog) in Monument Valley Park and then it was back to the office to fill Charlie in on Scott's and my meeting with Jeff Freeman.

Charlie, although he had reservations, said he was OK with Jeff's decisions about Priscilla Dalton and said he would immediately set up a meeting with Louisa Gardner, the school district's lawyer, to work out the details of the agreement and draft up a written document setting forth the terms, to be signed by Jeff and the school district, but not Priscilla Dalton. There was nothing in the agreement for her to consent to other than to provide coding tutoring for other students, and that's something she wanted to do in any event. And, since the agreement made no promises to her that she could legally enforce, including releases of potential liability, it would result in some uncertainty hanging over her life for a while, which would be a part of the punishment she deserved.

On Friday afternoon, McConnell Jones and Knight had a rare partnership meeting, starting at 4 p.m. Jennifer had been assigned the task of selecting an appropriate wine for the event and, going beyond her budgetary authorization, also bought a large jar of macadamia nuts from Hawaii. Bruce Jones, who has two kids in college, had called the meeting and set the usual agenda -- why are we working harder and making less money? We began the meeting, as was customary, with confessions about the pro bono work we were doing, or work we were doing at greatly reduced fees. I reported that I was helping a family facing foreclosure because of a billing error by a mortgage servicing company. Jennifer said she was helping a woman who was trying to buy a home but was running into problems due to inaccurate information in a credit report. Bruce confessed to representing a disabled veteran whose dog had been euthanized by a veterinarian because he didn't have the money to pay the veterinarian's fee.

On the positive side of the ledger, I was able to tell Bruce and Jennifer that I was spending a good amount of time helping Scott Freeman with his issues involving the Thurston Family Trust and that Scott (and, in part, his professional liability insurance company) were paying our charges on a timely basis. Jennifer said she was busy helping a well-established home building company complete the platting of fifty new home sites on the northeast side of town, and that billings for this work were being promptly paid. Bruce was representing a public company with a Colorado Springs office in the defense of a meritless age discrimination claim and, again, billings were timely paid.

We then turned to the usual discussion about how we could enhance our personal incomes from the practice of law without destroying life/work balance. The options were always the same. We could raise our rates, thereby making it harder for people who need our services to afford them. We could stop doing pro bono or reduced fee work for people who needed help and couldn't afford standard lawyer rates. We could eliminate a staff position or move some of our staff to part time, or reduce their salaries. We could scrap our current share-and-share-alike compensation arrangement and go to the kind of eat-what-you-kill plan most law firms use. Or, we could work harder and give up time with families, pets, charitable organizations, hobbies (including fishing), etc. Since none of these alternatives was acceptable, we ended the meeting, as we usually did, by finishing the wine (and most of the macadamia nuts) and reminding each other that we had a pretty good thing going with this little firm and we shouldn't mess it up.

On Saturday, after a catch-up-on-work morning in the office, Elsie and I headed to Denver to spend the night with Veronica at her LoDo condominium. This was Elsie's first visit to Veronica's home, and possibly her first ride in an elevator. She seemed to enjoy the elevator ride and she settled right into Veronica's condo, after a careful examination of all the places where her dog bed could be set up for the night. (She decided on Veronica's bedroom, at the foot of the bed, although the kitchen was a close second.)

Saturday evening, Veronica and I left Elsie at the condo and had dinner at a hole-in-the-wall restaurant a few blocks west of Veronica's building which served, as its specialty, fish tacos. I had been skeptical of fish tacos the first time I tried them, at the invitation of a friend, but have since come to like them. This was Veronica's first try at fish tacos and she found them, well, different, interesting, and not something she had previously encountered in her world travels. She doubted they could be found on the East Coast and concluded they were probably a Colorado culinary aberration.

After dinner we headed back east to Coors Field, a short half-mile walk, and took in a Rockies game. The Rockies were playing the Los Angeles Dodgers who, as usual, were running away with the National League West, thanks to a talented (and high-priced) pitching staff and a couple of home run hitting and base stealing outfielders. But this night, the Rockies were playing well and a rookie pitcher just brought up from Triple A Albuquerque was having a career game. At the end of five endings, he had struck out five and walked only one, and the Rockies were ahead 5 to 4.

During the break between the fifth and the sixth innings, Veronica surprised me with a question. She wanted me to explain the infield fly rule.

"Veronica, are you sure you want to do this?"

"Yes. If you want me to become a baseball fan, after talking me into buying a place to live within walking distance of Coors Field, I at least need to know the rules of the game. I'm a rules person, as you may have noticed."

"Well, OK, but I think this would be easier if you had more to drink."

"No. Go for it and let's see what happens."

"Alright. The rule works like this. It goes into effect if there are less than two outs and there are runners on first, or first and second, base. And the batter hits a fly ball that should be caught by an infielder, even if this means the infielder has to go aways out into the outfield to catch the ball. If all of that happens, then the umpire declares the batter to be out, whether or not the infielder catches the ball. The runners on base can advance at their peril, but they usually just stay put, at whatever base they are on."

"What in the world is the reason for a crazy rule like that?"

"If you didn't have this rule, the infielder could intentionally drop the ball and then start a double or triple play, which would basically be a sneaky trick, unfair to the team with runners on base."

"Well, I still think it's a crazy rule. This is clearly a guy thing and nothing women would ever think of. And while we're at it, tell me about the hidden ball trick."

"Wow, Veronica, I'm impressed that you've even heard of that. You don't see this very often in the major leagues because it's so embarrassing for the team that gets tricked. But I actually saw it happen here at Coors Field a few years ago, in a game against the Saint Louis Cardinals. So basically what happens is the first baseman holds onto the ball after a play, rather than throwing it back to the pitcher, as he usually does. The pitcher then acts as though he has the ball, even though he doesn't. If the runner on first base isn't paying attention and takes a leadoff from the base, the first baseman reaches over and tags him, and he's out."

"Another guy thing. Women would never allow that kind of behavior."

"Whatever. Are you ready to head home?"

"Yes. It's probably time to take Elsie down to the park for a last visit and then you can watch the rest of the game on television."

As was to be expected, the walk back to Veronica's condo required us to navigate our way around inebriated partiers along Blake Street, some of whom, as allowed by Colorado law, had guns in holsters around their waist in an apparent effort to look manly and important. This results in an occasional LoDo shooting, which seems to be the price people are willing to pay to ensure that their right to bear arms under the Second Amendment is not diminished. But tonight, everyone was well behaved.

After Elsie had her last pee down at the neighborhood park, which I was assigned to supervise, I watched the game on the television in Veronica's bedroom. I lasted through the eighth inning, after which I fell asleep. As I would learn in the morning, the Rockies went on to win the game by a score of ten to nine, with a dramatic walk off home run in the bottom of the ninth inning.

Sunday morning, I was up early, as usual, and headed to the kitchen in pursuit of coffee. There, I found a note on the kitchen counter. It said: "Jack, make me late for breakfast." I thereupon went back to bed and followed my instructions.

Veronica and I, and Elsie, hung out together until noon, reading the New York Times and comparing notes on the next week's events. (Elsie, of course, did not read the New York Times but she did chew on it a bit before we pulled it out of the plastic wrapper it was delivered in.) We still weren't sure what boots-on-the-ground assignments Ed had in mind for us, but whatever it was, it didn't seem to be something that would come to pass in the next week. We therefore didn't insert that into our respective schedules.

Elsie and I stopped at my office on the way back home in a further effort on my part to catch up on work.

Although the McConnell Jones & Knight lease prohibits pets in our office, our landlord is a dog guy who regularly brings his yellow Lab, Nyah, to his office, so I was comfortable that Elsie's hanging out with me for a couple of hours would not result in eviction.

Chapter 28

The following Tuesday was the day scheduled for our mediation in the Duane Thurston litigation. I went over to Scott's house for this event. I was wearing my usual lawyer uniform -- khaki pants, a blue button-down collar shirt, a tie displaying various famous trout flies, and a blue blazer, with most buttons intact. Scott was wearing the upscale workout clothes Stella had bought for him. Scott and I chatted a bit about what to expect in the mediation and then, using Scott's laptop, we signed on to the Zoom connection our mediator, Homer Weatherspoon, had set up for the mediation.

"Hello Judge. Jack McConnell with Scott Freeman, here in Colorado Springs. Thanks for taking on this matter." (It's customary in mediations where the mediator is a retired judge to refer to him or her as "Judge," even though he or she is no longer a sitting judge. This, in my experience, has a beneficial schmoozing effect.) On our Zoom connection screen, we could see that Weatherspoon was a large and distinguished looking Black man, with a deep and authoritative voice. He was wearing a dark blue suit with a white shirt and a handsome yellow bow tie. He had a short grey beard. He was pleasant and professional as he began our first session of the mediation, having already spent time with Duane Thurston and Manifort, who were in a separate conference room in Weatherspoon's offices.

"Good morning gentlemen, from Austin, where it's going to be 100 degrees today and with stagnant air. Well, I've read the material you sent me -- thanks for that -- and I think I know what's going on. This is certainly a bizarre lawsuit. I would have thought the primary plaintiff, Duane Thurston, would have been going after the estate of Maria Thurston or otherwise trying to challenge in court the decision she made to amend the trust agreement for the Thurston Family Trust. But, he and his lawyer apparently decided that, after Maria Thurston died and Scott became the successor trustee, there was no longer a way to challenge what Maria had done while she was trustee, and the only path available for a possible recovery was to sue Scott. And, as I understand it, the claim against Scott is that, while he was acting as Maria's lawyer, he failed to give Duane and his brother William notice that Maria was changing the trust agreement, which Duane Thurston and his lawyer say he should have done. And then, when Scott became the successor trustee after Maria's death, they say he had some kind of duty to ask a court, on their behalf as beneficiaries, to review Maria's right to amend the trust agreement. Something like that."

"Yes Judge," I said. "That's a good summary. And of course our position is that Scott appropriately represented Maria, while she was alive, as his client and he owed no duties to Duane Thurston or his brother. And after Maria's death, Scott's duty was to administer the Thurston Family Trust in accordance with the terms of the trust agreement, including the amendment Maria made that Duane Thurston is now complaining about and that substantially reduced his and his brother Billie's distributions from the trust. And it's our position that Maria had every right to do what she did under the terms of the trust agreement."

"Well, let's not spar about what the principles of law might be that are applicable to this case. Your judge could rule on those issues in any number of directions. He's an

OK judge, by the way. You could have done worse. But trying to predict his behavior in this case is just another variable that makes having this dispute resolved in a jury trial a form of irrational gambling. And Scott, as I'm sure you know, this lawsuit doesn't put the trust's assets at risk. It was designed to, and does, put your personal assets at risk. And as you have told me in your mediation statement, your errors and omissions insurance company hasn't yet agreed that you have insurance coverage if there's a judgment against you because the claims involve allegedly intentional acts. So, taking this case to trial requires you to put your personal net worth on the line -- home, cars, education accounts for your grand kids, vacation home in California, etc."

Scott stepped in at this point. "Judge, I, of course, understand all that but, as the now trustee of the Thurston Family Trust, I can't be using assets of the trust to resolve a claim against me personally. If there was ever a breach of fiduciary duty, that would be it."

"Well, you could probably dance around all that by deciding, as the successor trustee, that Maria did not have authority to amend the trust agreement in the first place."

"But Judge, she did have that authority and, as her lawyer while she was trustee, I told her she had that authority. And I'm not about to change my mind on any of that. This whole lawsuit is an exercise in extortion and I'm not going to allow Duane Thurston to pull that off."

Me: "So Judge, you've already spoken with Duane Thurston and his lawyer. What do they want to settle this case?"

Weatherspoon: "They want the amendment to the trust agreement that Maria made to be rescinded, with the effect that they receive the distributions out of the trust they would have received if Maria hadn't made the amendment. But, as a matter of settlement and compromise, Duane Thurston would agree to a distribution out of the trust to him and his brother, William, of twenty-five million dollars each in the form of PharmOne stock. Or, an equal amount in cash coming from the trust or from Scott."

At this point, even though I told Scott this is what we would be hearing from the mediator, I had the sense from his expression that he might be on his way to another cardiovascular accident, so it was time to take a break.

"Judge, give us ten minutes to talk about this and then bring us back."

"Right. I need to make a bathroom stop anyway."

"So Scott. Calm down. We've rehearsed this scene and, unless you've had a sudden change of mind, we know what our response is going to be -- tell Duane Thurston and Manifort to pound sand."

"I'm sorry McConnell. I promised myself I wouldn't let this get to me, but it does. After thirty-whatever years of trying to be a good, careful, caring, ethical, thoughtful lawyer, giving sound advice to clients, getting kicked around like this by the system I took an oath to uphold is hard to take."

"Well, that's what you get for choosing to go into the tranquil and disciplined world of estate planning. Now, if you had continued on as a litigator, which by the way you were very good at, you'd be accustomed to this sort of thing and it wouldn't upset you."

"Go to hell, McConnell. But no change of mind on my part. Stick with the game plan."

At precisely ten minutes after we started the break, Weatherspoon brought us back together again on the Zoom connection and asked if we had had enough time to caucus.

Me: "Yes Judge. Thanks. This is going nowhere. As Scott has said, he cannot, as a successor trustee of the Thurston Family Trust and an officer of the Thurston Family Foundation, and therefore a fiduciary, use assets of the Thurston Family Trust or Foundation to bargain away a claim against him personally. And he is firmly of the belief that he has not violated any duty he might have owed to Duane Thurston or Billie Thurston and he is unwilling to throw personal assets at someone he thinks is playing a game of extortion. So, our position on settlement is, as I told you in our mediation statement, a mutual dismissal of claims. We will dismiss our claims against Duane Thurston for abuse of process and malicious prosecution in exchange for a dismissal of his and Billie's claims against Scott. That's as far as we go."

Weatherspoon. "OK, well I'll convey that message to Duane and his lawyer, but this isn't going to settle the case. Duane Thurston, as best I can tell, is a gambler, and he'll take his chances with a hometown jury, meaning Scott's personal assets will continue to be at risk. Duane Thurston likes the idea of telling a jury that Scott Freeman set this whole thing up as a way to generate future lucrative employment opportunities for himself and his law firm."

Weatherspoon then left us alone in our virtual conference room and went off to talk with Duane and Manifort, where he would be doing what mediators do -- telling them Duane's claim was a loser and Scott's counterclaim was a winner and they'd better settle with a walkaway of claims on both sides while they had the chance.

(Mediators, not unlike trial court judges, learn early on that a good way to achieve a settlement is to tell both sides they're going to lose....)

Weatherspoon reconnected with us twenty minutes later and reported that Duane had reduced his settlement position to fifteen million for each himself and his brother, but that was his best and final offer. And, to inject some customary drama into the proceeding, Weatherspoon told us Duane and Manifort were packing up their briefcases and getting ready to leave.

"No Judge," I said. "That offer is unacceptable. Thanks for your efforts, but it's time to shut this mediation down and get on with preparing for a trial."

"Very well," Weatherspoon responded. "I'll prepare an email to both sides confirming that you have met your obligation to Judge Elefson to give mediation a good faith try. However, I'd encourage you to keep talking. As we've discussed, and as you very well know, taking this case to trial is a high stakes act of gambling involving unknown and unknowable odds." And with that final comment, he terminated the Zoom connection, leaving Scott and me together at Scott's home.

"Well McConnell, no surprises here. What do I need to be doing to prepare for a trial?"

"First, get healthy. Let's see if you can get that two miles a day up to three. Then, just continue to go back through your files and your time records, and revisit your reasons for concluding that Maria had the authority to amend the trust agreement to redirect funds from Duane and Billie to the Thurston Family Foundation. I'll be working on a trial brief, jury instructions, opening statement, witness examinations, and a closing argument. As you may recall

from your short time as a trial lawyer, the way you prepare
for a trial is to start with the closing argument and work
backwards, through the witness examinations, making sure
the evidence will be there to support the argument. After
that's all in place, you prepare an opening statement, telling
the jurors what the case is about and the evidence you intend
to present in support of the outcome you believe is correct.
I'll also get our expert witness up to speed and organize the
documents we plan to present at the trial. And I'll work with
Ed on a plan to learn what we can about Duane's possible
involvement in illegal drug trafficking. That's not spot-on
relevant to the claims being thrown at you but, on the good
guy/bad guy front -- always important in a jury trial -- I want
the jury to know why Maria did what she did. I expect
Manifort to object like crazy to that kind of evidence but I
think Judge Elefson will let it in. It will help to keep the
jurors awake and he's likely to be curious himself what
Duane Thurston might have been up to that caused Maria to
do what she did."

I then shook hands with Scott, in the way good
friends shake hands, and headed back to my office, where I
told Stephanie to get to work on travel plans to Austin for
Scott and me, and finding a reasonably priced hotel within
walking distance to the courthouse where we can hole up for
a week.

"What do you mean by 'reasonably priced'?"

"I don't know -- $100 a night?"

"You're delusional, but I'll do the best I can."

Since Linda, our receptionist, had done as instructed
and told everyone looking for me that I would be tied up all
day in a mediation, I bailed out early -- at 3:30 – and took
Elsie for a longer than usual walk up into Pike National

Forest. However, at around 5:00, as sometimes happens in the late spring in these parts, what had started out as a powder blue cloudless sky turned into a major thunderstorm, complete with drenching rain, abundant lightening and golf ball size hail. Elsie and I found a rock overhang where we could stay out of the wind and hail, and wait out the storm. Having learned the hard way to be prepared for this sort of thing, I had brought along a rain poncho and blanket large enough to cover both Elsie and me. Elsie was not happy about the thunder and huddled up next to me as close as she could get, putting her head on my lap and trying to cover her ears.

The storm raged on for the usual twenty minutes and then moved off to the east, toward downtown Colorado Springs. By 5:30, the sky was again blue and the wind had stopped and we were able to head back home without further adventure. Fortunately, I had put my SUV in the garage so it escaped the hail. But, the hail had stripped the leaves off many of the trees in my yard, which would likely invite disease and require a visit from the tree maintenance company that regularly takes a share of my disposable income. I made Elsie stay on the porch long enough for me to find a towel and wipe at least the first layer of mud off her oversized paws, and then we went inside, for her to have her dinner and me to have a glass of the house pinot noir.

Chapter 29

Ed called me in the morning at my office to compare notes. I told him the Duane Thurston mediation went nowhere, we were now in trial preparation mode, and the trial was a mere four weeks away. Other cases having docket priority over ours had settled, so we were sitting in first position, meaning the trial was likely to start on time. I also told him we were making progress on the Jeff Freeman internet defamation front and that Duane Thurston was indeed not the bad guy, as we had originally suspected. I also told him we were making no progress in regard to the ethical grievance Duane Thurston had filed with the Colorado Supreme Court through the Office of Attorney Regulation Counsel. That matter appeared to be headed to a hearing before a hearing board consisting of someone called the Presiding Disciplinary Judge and two members of something called the hearing board panel. I told Ed that Scott Freeman was making progress, albeit slowly, recovering from his open-heart surgery. He at least was up and about and walking a couple of miles a day.

"So Jack, as promised, I've been scratching around with regard to Duane Thurston's involvement in illegal drug activity and I've called in a few favors from people I've worked with in the past. This includes a former employee at NYZ Group. You may have read about this French company in the New York Times. It sells sophisticated spying and hacking equipment to multiple customers and has found itself on the wrong side of U.S. interests because some of its customers are not friends of our government. So, it has now been made subject to various U.S. sanctions, which it could probably care less about. In any event, it is regularly digging up information about drug trafficking, which is, of course, a worldwide phenomenon. I've also been in touch with a guy I know who was formerly a part of what the FBI calls the Joint Criminal Opioid and Darknet Enforcement Team. These people work with other agencies around the world in an effort to disrupt and dismantle the sale of illicit drugs and weapons. None of this has led to information about Duane Thurston directly. But I now have a better picture of what I think we should be looking for."

"And what is that?"

"Here's what seems to be going on, as we had suspected. The prescription pain killer meds -- mostly oxycontin, but there are others – that are making it onto the street are getting there through activities going on at the level of pharmacy benefit managers. As I told you, these companies position themselves as middlemen between drug manufacturers and health care plans, drug provider insurance plans and other big wholesale purchasers of prescription drugs. So, if someone is able to get a prescription for these pain meds, which is now hard to come by, the pills go from a manufacturer to a pharmacy benefit manager, on to a retail drug store or health plan or other drug dispensary, and ultimately to the prescription holder. The theory the FBI is now working on is that people inside pharmacy benefit manager operations are pulling a couple of pills out of each bottle of pain meds that is on its way to a legitimate wholesale customer and substituting in their place pills that look identical to the real thing. Pharmacists can't tell the difference between the real pills and the phony substitute pills, and patients, if it only happens a couple of times a bottle, also won't realize they are not getting the real thing.

The pills that are, by this process, taken out of the legitimate supply chain -- and this in total amounts to thousands of pills -- are then sold on the street to people who are addicted to the pain meds, can no longer get prescriptions, and are desperate."

"That's pretty scary."

"Yes, and as you probably know, drug overdoses have killed more than 100,000 people a year, just in the US, and the majority of those deaths involve drugs purchased on the street, which are sometimes laced with fentanyl, a really powerful synthetic opioid that is cheap to make. Street drug purchasers can't identify fentanyl when they make a purchase, and sometimes they're even looking for it in a desperate attempt to get relief from their craving."

"So do we know which pharmacy benefit managers are involved in this scheme?"

"Not for sure, but in your part of the country the FBI has been homing in on a company having an operation in Littleton, Colorado, called ExpressRX. We have no direct evidence that this company is involved, but the FBI was able to monitor suspicious cryptocurrency transactions tied to it that look like the laundering of illegal drug trafficking money."

"And again, no link to Duane Thurston?"

"No. But one of the women Duane Thurston was living with and who accused him of physically abusing her, Angela Forrester, is a former employee of ExpressRX and I think she may be our connect-the-dots link to tie Duane Thurston with ExpressRX and the street sale of prescription pain meds."

"And?"

"So this is where you and Veronica put boots on the ground. Angela Forrester is now a pharmacist in Littleton working at, of all places, a PharmOne store. She lives in Littleton and is a regular patron at a Littleton bar called the Cheval Blanc, not far from where she lives. Probably three days a week, she heads for this bar after work and has a lonely happy hour all by herself."

"How do you know all that?"

"Jack, you remember there are parts of my business I can't tell you about. This is one of them."

"And?"

"You and Veronica need to show up at the Cheval Blanc and confront her about ExpressRX's involvement in this supply-chain-to-street activity and Duane Thurston's possible connection with that activity."

"Well that's great, but what's going to keep her from shouting 'Security!' and having some 250 pound bouncer pin us to the ground and have us hauled away by the police?"

"We've had this conversation before but, as you may recall, people in the espionage business -- which is what we're doing here -- learned long ago that there are two ways to recruit agents -- spies. One is money. A promise of lots of money followed by a new identity in a faraway place. The other is -- I hate to use the term but there is no other -- blackmail. A threat to reveal information the person being recruited desperately wants to keep private. Blackmail is the more successful alternative. Here, we know something about Angela Forrester that she very much wants to keep private. And before you meet with her, I'll let you know what that is. Your and Veronica's assignment will then be to cut a deal with her that this information will remain private

provided she tells us what we want to know about
ExpressRX's and Duane Thurston's involvement in the
diversion of prescription pain meds to the street."

"I don't think I like this Ed. Is this legal?"

"Do you want to help Scott?"

"Of course."

"Then let's again defer your question to another
time."

"And why does Veronica have to be involved in
this? Why can't I just wander into the Cheval Blanc looking
for lonely chicks and keep Veronica out of this?"

"No offense Jack, but you're too old to be picking
up chicks in a bar and Veronica was way better than you at
playing her part in the drama we put together to solve the
counterfeit cashier's check case. She has real talent for this
sort of thing. You, I'm afraid, don't. And, anyway, I think
Angela Forrester is going to be more willing to open up to a
woman than a lecherous, ogling sixty-year-old male. Angela
Forrester, by the way, is quite attractive. I'll send you a
couple of photos."

"I still don't like this."

"You do, do you not, want to go into the trial of
Duane Thurston's lawsuit armed with evidence that Maria
Thurston was right when she decided Duane Thurston was a
bad guy and shouldn't get a huge chunk of money --
generated by Andy's hard work -- out of the Thurston
Family Trust?"

"Yes."

"So this is your best shot. It may not work but --
nothing ventured nothing gained."

"OK, I'll get with Veronica and tell her I'm going to
treat her to drinks at a place she's never heard of -- the

Cheval Blanc in Littleton -- and see when her schedule will permit this event. Do we know which days of the week Angela heads for this bar after work?"

"Best guess is later in the week -- Wednesday, Thursday, Friday."

After my call with Ed, I put in a call to Veronica on an encrypted cell phone she uses for private conversations that are not supposed to be subject to possible eavesdropping, including by her employer, the Fed. I told her briefly what Ed had told me and asked her to let me know what her schedule looked like for the following week. I told her we'd work out the details of our attempt at espionage over the weekend when she was planning to come down to Colorado Springs in any event. Veronica's tone of voice implied skepticism but she did not, as she has been known to do, tell me Ed and I were out of our minds.

My next call was to Charlie Justin. He told me he and the school district's lawyer, Louisa Gardner, had, after much back and forth, managed to come up with an acceptable draft of an agreement between Jeff Freeman and the school district setting forth the terms under which Jeff would agree not to sue the district. The main sticking point in the negotiations had to do with the requirement that the district must cause InstaFlip to remove the reputation-damaging post about Jeff and publish a retraction, and the requirement that the district had to come up with a viable plan to shut down internet search requests picking up the original post. But, to her credit, Louisa Gardner had thrown enough legal threats at InstaFlip to achieve its full and complete cooperation. The draft agreement had been circulated to the school board members who, as anticipated, were unhappy about the entire Jeff Freeman affair and wanted to fire someone but weren't sure who. In the end, however, they finally came around to realizing their best bad choice under the circumstances was to go along with Jeff's demands and keep things as quiet as possible. The board, therefore, had authorized the superintendent of schools -- the district's CEO -- to sign the settlement agreement.

Veronica finally made it to Colorado Springs around 8:00 p.m. on Friday, looking exhausted (but still beautiful). As usual, there had been a multi-car accident in the Gap shortly before Monument Hill that brought southbound traffic on I-25 to a halt for thirty minutes. I had dinner and a glass of chardonnay waiting for her, and Elsie gave her a big welcome-back lick and wag. We agreed we would defer further discussion about going into espionage mode until morning. After dinner, I tucked Veronica into bed, without distraction (although a therapeutic back rub, and front rub, certainly crossed my mind), and she promptly went into a deep rapid eye movement sleep, interrupted only by an occasional snore.

Saturday morning, I spent some time in the office starting the ramp up for the trial of Duane Thurston's lawsuit against Scott. I then put in a call to Scott, who was -- good for him -- out on a therapeutic heart surgery recovery walk but with cell phone in hand. I first told him that Jeff Freeman's terms of settlement with the school district were on track, and that Jeff would be back in the classroom next week. I then passed on what Ed had told me about ExpressRx and Angela Forrester. I told him Veronica and I were planning a confrontation with Ms. Forrester at the Cheval Blanc in Littleton sometime during the next week.

"McConnell, I engaged you as a lawyer, not a private investigator or a spy. What the hell are you up to?"

"Scott, McConnell Jones and Knight is a full service law firm. We do whatever we need to do to further our clients' interests."

"Yeah, but that doesn't mean risking your or Veronica's mysterious disappearance -- and, by the way, I never engaged Veronica to do anything."

"Well, we're a team and this will all be fine. We just need to generate a little circumstantial evidence to the effect that Maria Thurston was correct in deciding Duane Thurston was a bad guy and that the assets of the Thurston Family Trust, generated from Andy's entrepreneurship, would be better used to further the purposes of the Thurston Family Foundation rather than being doled out to Duane to support frivolous, or illegal, activity. Again, our position at trial is going to be that Maria did not need any specific justification to change the distribution terms of the trust agreement, but the jury is still going to want to know that she had good reasons for giving Duane, and Billie, the haircut her amendment to the trust agreement gave them."

"OK, but if you and Veronica get yourselves killed, I'm denying any responsibility."

"Got it. Agreed. Finish your walk. I'll let you know what happens."

Chapter 30

Veronica and I had decided we would make our trip to the Cheval Blanc the following Thursday. I picked her up at her condominium at around 4:00 and we headed west to Littleton. Veronica had changed into workout clothes and donned a Rockies hat I had given her. I stayed mostly in my lawyer uniform but took off my tie. Cooper was home from college for the weekend so, via a text message (I was getting better at these...), I left him in charge of Elsie. I told him I wouldn't be back until after her dinner time and to feed her and give her an after dinner walk around the neighborhood. To further his enthusiasm for this assignment, I told him he could invite Amy along for the walk.

Veronica and I made it to the Cheval Blanc at around 4:30. It was a neighborhood pub kind of establishment, with a large wooden horse, painted white, in front. The paint was peeling off the horse in several places, suggesting it had been there for a while and had perhaps lived through a few hailstorms. The inside of the Cheval Blanc had wood paneling and typical bar furniture, and the lights were dimmed, in traditional bar fashion. The actual bar was maybe thirty feet long and looked like it had been imported from some Old-World pub in Scotland, although the bartender told us it had actually been made in Des Moines. Said bartender, looking like someone needing a second job to pay rent until his band made its first hit recording, was the only person waiting on the small number of customers at this early hour. Veronica and I found a table off to the side of the room with a good view of the front door, and ordered the house chardonnay, which was better than expected.

Angela Forrester walked in at just before 5:00. We immediately recognized her from the photos Ed had sent us. She was wearing nice fitting medical scrubs -- which seem to have become the fashion hit of the decade -- in a light blue color. She was indeed attractive. Maybe fifty years old. Hair cut short. Tall. Slender. Nice body (my opinion, not Veronica's). But her face wore signs of stress. She headed right to the bar and obviously knew the bartender from prior visits. We couldn't hear her words exactly but it sounded like she ordered "the usual," which turned out to be a gin drink of some sort.

After Angela had settled in for a few minutes, Veronica moved to a bar stool next to her.

"Hello Angela."

"I beg your pardon. Do I know you?"

"No. But I know you, and we need to talk. My name is Veronica. I think this would work best if you came with me to my table off to the side here."

Angela, with hesitation, followed Veronica to the table where I was still sitting.

"This is my friend Jack. We are here and wanting to talk to you because a friend of ours is being sued by Duane Thurston in a lawsuit in Texas and the case is due to go to trial in a few weeks."

"I guess I'll never be rid of that man."

"Jack is our friend's lawyer. I'm just a friend. But let's get right to the point. We know you had a live-in relationship with Duane Thurston down in Texas and you reported to the police in Austin on two occasions that he had physically abused you. After the second such event, your relationship ended. Thurston was eventually charged with assault and entered into a plea bargain that kept him out of jail."

"How do you know these things?"

"We have our ways, and let me just say they are very thorough. But to get to the matter of consequence for us, we believe Duane Thurston has been involved in a criminal enterprise that diverts prescription pain meds onto the street -- and that this involves ExpressRX and you have knowledge about the enterprise. That's what we want to talk with you about."

"Wait a minute. What the hell is going on here? And why should I talk to you?"

"You need to talk to us because we know some things about your past that we believe you would not like to have disclosed. Does the name Gregory Roberts mean anything to you?"

"No. Should it?"

"In the press, ten years ago now, Gregory Roberts became known as the Angel of Death. He was accused of facilitating twenty-three suicides of allegedly terminally ill people in Colorado and he was charged with homicides for each of those deaths. Before he could be tried, however, he took his own life. All of these deaths, including Roberts' own death, involved a fatal drug cocktail which included high doses of prescription pain meds and fentanyl. However, the police were never able to determine where Roberts got those drugs. We believe you were involving in supplying the drugs."

"That's ridiculous. How dare you make those accusations."

"Well Angela," it was my turn to speak, "you need to listen to this recording." At this point I took out a small recording device and played a mini-cassette tape Ed had sent to me.

"Angie, this is Greg. I need another shipment. I'll pick it up at the usual place at the usual time, on the 16th Street mall. As soon as I have the meds, I'll make the transfer into your account."

"OK. Tomorrow at 4:30."

At this point, Angela, notwithstanding a generous application of makeup, turned an ashen shade of white, put her head down, and began to cry.

"What do you want with me?" she was finally able to say.

"A bargain, of sorts," I said. "If you tell us what you know about Duane Thurston's involvement in getting prescription pain meds onto the street, we'll give you the tape you just heard. There is only one copy and it's right here."

"Why should I trust you?"

"Because you have no other choice."

"Can I have another drink?"

"Of course. Our treat." Veronica then went over to the bar and told the bartender to whip up another "the usual" for Angela.

"OK, I guess you're right. I have no other choice. And I guess I knew this day would come. So here's all I know. One night when Duane Thurston was drunk or high on drugs and getting ready to beat me up, he boasted he had a deal going with someone at ExpressRX that was paying him lots of money. He said the deal involved taking prescription pain meds out of their original shipping containers and substituting look-alike fakes. The real drugs then made it onto the street and generated big profits. He said he got a share of the profits because, through the contacts he had at ExpressRX, he had been instrumental in setting up the fake-for-real strategy, and this was his payback."

"You worked at ExpressRX for a while, right? Did you know this was going on?"

"No. Thurston got me the job at ExpressRX and, at his request, I introduced him to people who worked there, although he already knew many of these people because he was regularly dealing with Express RX on behalf of PharmOne. I had no involvement in this divert-to-the-street operation. Anyway, after Duane got done beating up on me that night and demanding sex, he said he would kill me if I told anyone what he had just told me. And I took his threat seriously -- and still do."

Angela was well into her second drink at this point, and was still wiping her eyes. Veronica, who will forever be a nurturing and caring person, put her arm around Angela and told her it would all be OK.

"One last question, Angela, and then this tape is yours. Did Duane Thurston say who his primary contact was at ExpressRX for this divert-to-the-street enterprise?"

"No. But in this drunken tirade I'm telling you about, he mentioned the name Trevor, and that it would be Trevor who killed me if I said anything."

"All right. Here's the tape," I said. "We wish you no harm. As far as we're concerned, this conversation never occurred. Can we give you a ride home?"

"Thanks, but it's only a short walk and God knows I need a walk. And I don't think I want to be seen with you.

You know, it's strange, but it helps, after all this time, to talk about what went on down there in Austin. I've had plenty of bad times in my life, but that was probably the worst. I hope your friend can avoid whatever poison Duane Thurston is throwing his way."

Veronica and I then settled up on Angela Forrester's and our bar tab, and escorted her out the door of the Cheval Blanc. Out on the sidewalk, Veronica gave Angela a small hug and we left her to continue on her own. Since it seemed like the right lawyerly thing to do, I gave her my business card and told her to call me if she had any follow-up thoughts from our conversation. Veronica and I then returned to my SUV and headed east on I-470, back to Veronica's condominium.

"Good job, Veronica. Ed was right. You really do have a talent for espionage."

"I feel sorry for her. She is trapped in a scary circumstance thanks to her relationship with Duane Thurston."

"I agree. But we all need to live with the choices we make in life. And, in that regard, we need to live up to our part of the bargain to the effect that this conversation never occurred."

Although I was tempted to stay the night at Veronica's condo, I knew I had to get home to Elsie so I dropped Veronica off with a hug and a kiss and headed back south on I-25 to Colorado Springs. I was tempted to call Ed on my cell phone on the trip home but, since my SUV predates hands free telephone technology and I didn't like talking on the phone while I was driving, I turned on KOA and listened to the Rockies game. The Rockies were in Atlanta playing the Braves and, as usual, the Rockies' bullpen had blown a comfortable lead and they were now well on their way to another road game loss.

The I-25 south bound traffic was its usual late afternoon stop and go, and I finally made it home at 7:30. It was a warm late spring evening and Elsie and Cooper -- and Amy -- were on the porch when I pulled in the driveway. Elsie bounded down off the porch to give me a welcome home greeting. I thanked Cooper and Amy for looking after Elsie, took custody of their beer cans, and sent them on their way back home. I then took Elsie inside, poured myself a chardonnay, popped a frozen pizza in the microwave and put in a call to Ed on his encrypted phone.

"Hello Ed. I think our meeting with Angela Forrester went well. Veronica, as you said, does indeed have talent for boots on the ground espionage." I then told him about our encounter with Angela Forrester at the Cheval Blanc.

"Good. What's back on my plate?"

"I need you, in whatever way you do this sort of thing, to get the last name of an ExpressRX employee named Trevor. He's the guy Duane Thurston has hooked up with in connection with the diversion-to-the-streets prescription drug scheme."

"Ok, I'm on it. For someone in my line of work, that should be easy. But what are you going to do with this information?"

"I'm going to designate Trevor as a witness in the trial of Duane Thurston's lawsuit against Scott and lay on him a subpoena to testify. And then we'll see what happens."

Chapter 31

In the morning, I headed to the office early since, Stephanie told me, the work I had been neglecting was piling up. But before taking on other projects, I put in a call to Scott and gave him further details about the meeting with Angela Forrester. He, as usual, told me to march on in preparing for the upcoming trial, and to be careful. He said his heart surgeon, Dr. McCann, had given him a "doing OK" report and told him he was sufficiently recovered from his operation to make the trip to Texas for the trial. But, she said, don't jump back into full stress mode.

"So Jack, remind me what I should be doing to prepare for this trial."

"As I previously told you, you need to do the same things you did to prepare for your deposition -- look through your files and your time records, and brush up on why you told Maria she had the authority to change the trust agreement for the Thurston Family Trust after Andy's death, what she told you were her reasons for changing the trust agreement, and why you didn't tell Duane and Billie that Maria was changing the agreement to reduce their distributions. You should also read the transcript from your deposition so your testimony at the trial will be consistent with your deposition testimony. As you know, one of the games trial lawyers like to play is to trick a witness into saying something at a trial that is different from what the witness said in a deposition. Then, the lawyer whips out a transcript of the deposition and goes into a rant that the witness is talking out of both sides of his mouth -- saying one thing in a deposition, while under oath, and saying something different at a trial, while under oath. So, members of the jury, the witness can't be trusted to tell the truth about anything."

"Do you guys still do that sort of thing?"

"Of course we do. Credibility is everything in a jury trial. You may recall -- I certainly do -- you played that trick on one of my witnesses thirty-whatever years ago during the trial where we first met. And which, you may also recall, you lost."

"Well, that wasn't my fault. I had bad facts to deal with and even worse law."

"I agree, and you did a masterful job playing the cards you were dealt. It wasn't your fault that the jury didn't like your client."

"Neither did I."

Ed got back to me on Wednesday. Trevor's last name was Sheffield. He was a licensed pharmacist with a degree in pharmacology from the University of Denver. His license was first issued fifteen years ago. No record of any disciplinary action. He had been working for ExpressRX for ten years and was now a vice president in charge of distribution. No criminal record other than a DUI a couple of years ago. The DUI arrest involved drugs and not alcohol. He paid a hefty fine and was given a deferred sentence and one year of probation. Ed, as usual, didn't tell me how Trevor's last name and the other information he gave me was obtained, and I had learned not to ask.

I told Stephanie to prepare a subpoena requiring Sheffield to appear, by video, and testify at the trial of Duane Thurston's lawsuit against Scott, but I told her to hold off serving the subpoena until ten days prior to the trial, at which time I would endorse him as a witness and do my best to fend off Manifort's objection to this eve-of-trial endorsement of a new witness. I would, as we always do in these circumstances, tell the judge the witness was needed to rebut new evidence we just learned the plaintiff was intending to present.

The next three weeks flew by as I worked to keep other clients under control, prepare for Scott's trial, and give Elsie her customary walks and stick throws. (She, I had learned, preferred sticks to tennis balls; frisbees were a distant second.) I did, however, find a day when I could head up to the west end of Eleven Mile Canyon, where we had spread RJ's and Abby's ashes, and catch a few fish. This time of year, the river gets crowed early, so I left home at 6:00 and had staked out my space by 7:00, just as the sun was making its way into the canyon and onto the water. While waiting for the sun to reach the water, I thought about RJ and the many days we had spent at this very spot enjoying our friendship, having RJ show me his techniques, and teaching these fish to be careful what they ate. I missed RJ terribly and good memories didn't fill the bill. But, as he would have told me, life goes on.

When I arrived at the river, the trout were already busy grazing on tiny little mayflies. I hooked up with half a dozen nice fish and then the feeding suddenly stopped, just as a crowd of other fishermen started to encroach on my location. I then decided it was time to move on. My usual strategy in Eleven Mile Canyon was to fish the upper part of the river, which is catch and release only, early in the day and then move down stream to the part of the river where a small number of fish can be harvested. There are fewer fish in this part of the river, but there are also fewer fishmen, and it's still a beautiful stretch of water. I caught another four fish, this time using flies -- including my recently tied Adams 12's -- that were actually big enough to see. All in all, a good morning of fishing. However, at 11:00, it was back to the office to continue putting the pieces together for the trial.

Even though the lawsuit filed by Duane Thurston would involve only a handful of witnesses and a small number of documents, there was still much work to be done to prepare for the trial. I needed to draft a trial brief, telling the judge what our position was and what we believed were the rules of law applicable to the case. I needed to adopt a strategy for jury selection -- what kind of people did we want on the jury? I needed to prepare an opening statement wherein I would tell the jurors what the evidence would be that would be presented to them during the trial, and the significance of that evidence. I needed to prepare the direct examination of our expert witness, Regina Ramirez. I needed to prepare cross examinations for Duane Thurston and his expert witness. I needed to prepare the testimony of Trevor Sheffield, although I fully expected he would find a way to avoid his subpoena and not have to testify. I needed to prepare what I thought the jury instructions for the case should be. I needed to prepare a closing argument, being sure I'd have the evidence necessary to support the argument.

During the time I was in full-speed-ahead trial preparation mode, the Fed sent Veronica back to Venezuela where the S.O.S.-related attack on that country's banking system had come back to life. We stayed in touch with emails, text messages and Facetime calls, but we had to be careful in our communications since, in all probability, they were being monitored -- by somebody.

Scott and I headed to Texas on the Sunday before the trial was to begin. We flew into Houston, one of the few places having a direct flight from Colorado Springs. We then drove to Austin in a wheezy little four banger rental car and settled into the extended stay hotel that Stephanie had chosen for us. It was clean, comfortable and functional, and only three blocks from the courthouse where the trial would take place. But, if I ever again found myself in need of a long term stay in Austin, Texas, this probably wouldn't be the place I would pick.

Scott did OK on our trip, but he was clearly tired by the time we got to our destination. We spent an hour Sunday afternoon going over our game plan and then we went across the street to a Mexican restaurant and had a nice, not too spicey, dinner and went to bed early.

On Monday morning, we arrived at the courthouse at 8:30, as we had been instructed to do by Sue Ann, Judge Elefson's clerk. The courthouse was a modern building and the courtroom where our trial would take place was also modern, with large video monitors and microphones hanging from the ceiling in multiple locations.

The first matter at hand was a meeting with Judge Elefson in his chambers -- his office --just outside the courtroom. Since this meeting was a lawyers only event, I left Scott in the court room and headed into Judge Elefson's chambers. Manifort was already there, in the waiting area, and he declined a proffered handshake. Manifort was wearing a coat and tie, and a Dallas Cowboys logoed necktie. I had put on a suit for this occasion -- one of the two I owned (and newly dry cleaned for the trial) -- a white button-down collar shirt, and a conservative striped tie carrying no political, sports team loyalty, fishing, or other message.

Judge Elefson then invited us into his office -- he had not yet put on his robe -- and, as was customary behavior for trial court judges, he asked us if there was some way we could settle this case and avoid the need for a trial. Manifort and I assured him we had explored settlement but that this was one of those cases that needed to be tried. I used this time with the judge to explain to him that Scott Freeman had no flexibility to settle. He was now the trustee of the Thurston Family Trust and the chief executive officer of the Thurston Family Foundation and, as a fiduciary, he couldn't be putting the assets of either the trust or the foundation on the table in pursuit of a settlement of a lawsuit that had been brought against him personally. And, he wasn't about to use his family's assets to settle claims he felt were groundless and an exercise in extortion. Judge Elefson said he understood settlement was not to be had and told us the process of jury selection would begin promptly at 1:00 pm. He told us we had three days to complete the trial. Otherwise, we would be in conflict with his criminal docket and things would get chaotic. Scott and I headed off to a nearby Starbucks where we further discussed our game plan for jury selection.

At precisely 10:38, while Scott and I were still at Starbucks, I received a text message from Judge Elefson's clerk, Sue Ann, marked urgent, and telling me I needed to return to the courthouse immediately. Scott and I did as instructed. I again left Scott in the courtroom and went into Judge Elefson's chambers. Manifort was there. Sue Ann was there. Judge Elefson looked ashen, as did Sue Ann and Manifort.

"Mr. McConnell, there will be no trial today. Duane Thurston is dead. His body was found this morning by a housekeeper when she came to work. The police were called and the cause of death is believed to be a drug overdose -- a lethal amount of fentanyl loaded into recreational cocaine. However, an autopsy will be needed to confirm this. Mr. Manifort has told me co-plaintiff William Thurston is in no position to proceed with this lawsuit on his own, so I am vacating the trial. I also received this morning a motion to quash a subpoena you served on someone named Trevor Sheffield. I'm granting that motion since there will be no trial. I'll count on you lawyers to figure out what happens next. Perhaps Duane Thurston's estate will want to continue with the lawsuit, but that's obviously not something in my control. I must say, in fifteen years on the bench, I've never had anything like this happen. In all events, I'll tell the jury commissioner that I won't be needing a panel of prospective jurors for this case. Please keep me informed of your further decisions. What a strange business this is. You're excused."

Manifort and I nodded and left Judge Elefson's chambers without further dialogue, and we made no attempt to discuss "what happens next." Back in the courtroom, I caught up with Scott and told him what had occurred.

"Jack, they took him out. This was not a typical overdose by a desperate addict who could no longer get a prescription for pain meds or someone doing recreational cocaine. This was an assassination. By subpoenaing Trevor Sheffield to testify in this trial, you got too close to the nest. Whoever is behind this diversion of prescription pain meds to the street could not allow Thurston, or Sheffield, to testify at a trial. With 100,000 a year overdose deaths in this country, this is a perfect murder. No one will ever find out how Thurston received the drugs that killed him. The conclusion will be that he was looking for a cocaine high and got a bad batch of cocaine, laced with fentanyl, from some street drug vendor. Happens every day. Just another statistic."

"You may be right, Scott. You've told me Maria thought Duane was using cocaine, and maybe even dealing it. We now know there was much more to his involvement with illicit drugs. I'll probably get over it but, you know, at the moment I'm feeling like I caused Duane Thurston's death."

"That's nonsense. What did your mother do to you to instill in you this deep-seated need to always feel guilty about something?"

"I've often wondered that myself. I think it had something to do with her being a die-hard Republican devoted to Richard Nixon. In any event, let's get out of here and head back to Houston, and see if we can find a flight back to Colorado Springs." We then checked out of the hotel, fought the traffic back to Houston, remembered to fill the rental car's gas tank and dumped the rental car at the return location. On the drive back to Houston, I called Stephanie and asked her to try to book us a flight to Colorado Springs at whatever outrageous last minute air fare we would have to pay. She found us seats on a United flight leaving Houston at 5:30. Our seats were in first class, since that's all that was left. Scott didn't like the idea of having to pay for first class transportation for himself and his lawyer, but I reminded him he was saving lots of money by our being able to leave Austin earlier than planned and not having to pay our expert witness, Regina Ramirez, her full fee for testifying. I also put in a call to Regina and told her of Duane Thurston's death and that the trial had been cancelled. I told her to invoice me for the work she had done preparing for the trial and that I would promptly get her paid upon receipt of her invoice.

I then called Ed and left him a voice mail on his secure cell phone telling him of the day's surprise events. Just as we were getting ready to board our flight, Ed called back and reported another surprise. Trevor Sheffield was dead. His body was found in a local park in Littleton where drug trafficking is a regular occurrence. The police department in Littleton is treating this as another drug overdose death. Cocaine laced with fentanyl. Happens every day. Not worth a serious investigation.

On the flight back to Colorado Springs, after accepting United Airlines' first class only invitation for a glass (actually two) of merlot, Scott and I tried to start untangling the what-happens-next knots. Our first topic of conversation had to do with our own, and Veronica's and Ed's, safety. Were any of us now too close to the nest to be on somebody's hit list? We concluded we were not. Ed was an expert at being invisible. So he was safe. And it seemed to us highly unlikely that the criminals at the top of the prescription-drugs-diverted-to-the-street chain of command would conclude that Scott or I ever acquired enough information to jeopardize their operation (although my having issued a subpoena to Sheffield might get someone's attention). In any event, we concluded that, with Duane Thurston and Trevor Sheffield out of the way, the trail was cold. We also felt our meeting with Angela Forrester was sufficiently discrete that we hadn't put her, or Veronica, in harm's way. However, Angela Forrester might still be hanging out because of her relationship with Duane

Thurston. There wasn't anything we could do to make that go away. But, I would make sure she knew about Thurston's and Sheffield's deaths. She would have to deal with that information as she saw fit. Despite our feeling that Scott and Veronica and I were safe from a drug cartel murder, we agreed that doors should be locked and vigilance exercised.

Our flight to Colorado Springs arrived on time, notwithstanding typical spring thunderstorms over the Front Range. I retrieved my SUV at the airport, took Scott home and told him we would regroup later in the week to further explore "what happens next." I then picked up Elsie at the home of her friend, Buttercup, a slightly neurotic Irish setter who lived down the street from us and where she had been staying while I was gone, and we headed back to my house. Elsie, in the tradition of Fletcher, seemed disappointed that her sleep over with Buttercup had ended but she gave me a friendly "OK, you're my person" lick and wag, settled into her dog bed in my bedroom and slept through the night. I made myself a sandwich with some cheese and left-over chicken I found in the refrigerator, poured myself a glass of the house merlot, and watched the Rockies blow another late inning lead against San Diego. Before I crawled into bed, I sent Veronica, who was still in Venezuela, a cryptic text message telling her the Duane Thurston trial had been cancelled and asking her to call me when she had access to a secure connection. I then went to bed and endured a night of disrupting thoughts driven by a day of unanticipated events.

Chapter 32

On Thursday, two days after cancellation of the trial and our return to Colorado Springs, Scott and I hooked up for lunch at a heart-healthy Vietnamese restaurant in downtown Colorado Springs to further pursue the what-happens-next agenda. One matter that was clear (as such things go) is that, under the trust agreement for the Thurston Family Trust, if a beneficiary dies and has no spouse or children, any undistributed interest the beneficiary had in the trust is terminated and rolls over to the Thurston Family Foundation. So, Duane's estate couldn't claim the interest in the trust he would have had if he hadn't died. However, this might not prevent Duane's estate from pursuing the claim against Scott that Duane had been asserting in the Texas lawsuit. The claim, as presented by Duane's estate, would be that, but for Maria's amendment to the trust agreement, facilitated by Scott, Duane would already have received $30 million in PharmOne stock and that stock would be a part of his estate, available to pay creditor claims and make distributions to devisees named in a will or to heirs at law under Texas statutes dealing with a death without a will – an intestate death.

"So Scott, what do you know about Duane's estate planning?"

"Nothing really. Maria told me he had never bothered to sign a will, meaning he probably died intestate. If that's correct, since he had no spouse and his parents are dead, his siblings – Billie and Phillip – would be his heirs. But we have no idea what kind of estate he might have.

Based on what Maria has told me about how Duane lived his life, my guess is his liabilities exceed his assets. In any event, if I'm right that Duane in fact had no will, I think it makes sense to have Phillip try to get himself appointed as Duane's personal representative and then proceed to administer Duane's estate in a probate proceeding under Texas law. Phillip won't have a clue how to do that, but I'll hook him up with a Texas lawyer who can handle the details of estate administration. Despite what lawyers try to make people believe, probate is a pretty simple process. The personal representative collects the assets, pays the liabilities, and distributes what's left to the devisees if there's a will and to the heirs at law if there's not. However, one little wrinkle here may be that, if Duane has left behind a ton of debts, one or more of his creditors could decide to try to control the administration of his estate in pursuit of getting paid."

"Am I right that having Phillip serve as personal representative would eliminate the chance that Duane's estate would continue to pursue a claim against you?"

"Maybe. As personal representative, Phillip would never conclude that having Duane's estate continue to sue me would have any useful purpose. On the other hand, if one of Duane's creditors gets appointed as personal representative, that creditor might decide the path to getting paid includes pursuing the claim Duane started against me and carrying on with Duane's strategy of extortionate litigation. Or, a creditor could go after Phillip if he's the personal representative and demand that he pursue the claim against me. But, all of that seems unlikely, so I'm going to move on and find things to worry about other than Duane

Thurston's lawsuit. Bottom line, I think the Texas lawsuit is history. However, we can't know that for sure until a personal representative for Duane's estate has been appointed and creditor claims are filed. At some point down the road, after the dust settles on the administration of Duane's estate and assuming there are no surprises, you're going to need to ask Manifort to dismiss the lawsuit against me. I'll let you know when the time comes to do that."

Assuming the Texas lawsuit wouldn't be coming back to life, Scott's biggest what-happens-next problem then became what to do with Billie. Although Maria tried to play an important role in Billie's life, Duane had gotten in the way of that, with the effect that Billie had come to rely solely on Duane to take care of his needs – manage his assets and liabilities, see to his doctors' appointments, keep him out of trouble generally, and otherwise keep his life organized, all the while using Billie's money from the trust for an occasional personal loan, never to be repaid. Earlier in the day, Scott had gone to see Billie and told him of Duane's death. Scott said Billie didn't seem surprised by this, as though he somehow knew Duane had been swimming in dangerous waters. Scott told Billie he and Stella would help to take up the slack and assist him in dealing with life's details.

Although, because of his diminished capacity, Billie was no doubt in a situation where a court-appointed conservator could be put in place to handle his finances and a court-appointed guardian could be put in place to oversee his other needs, Scott knew very well these court supervised strategies for dealing with what the law rudely calls an "impaired" person are unsatisfactory, resulting in a huge expense and leaving the impaired person confused, humiliated and depressed.

Scott said he and Stella had decided, as Maria would have wanted, that they could cobble together a support team to help Billie without the need for court involvement, to include a plan to nurture his talents as an artist. Scott also said he had met with Phillip and told him of his half-brother's death. Again, no surprise on Phillip's part. He was never close to Duane and shared Maria's belief that he might have been involved in illegal drug-related activity. The silver lining to the clouds caused by Duane's death would appear to be that Phillip could now nurture a relationship with his other half-brother, Billie, something Duane's control over Billie's life had prevented.

Scott and I had one other what-happens-next issue to discuss. Should the information we had acquired about ExpressRX, and Duane Thurston and Trevor Sheffield, unverified though it was, be turned over to some federal drug crimes agency? We concluded that, as lawyers, we had an ethical duty to do that. The question then became – how should that information be shared without putting Angela Forrester in harm's way? We thought about asking Veronica to be the communicator – one government agent to another government agent, subject to promises of confidentiality. But we finally decided the best bad choice available to us was to have Ed, through his contact with the former FBI guy who had been involved in the Joint Criminal Opioid and Darknet Enforcement enterprise, obliquely make the information transfer, planting the seed that perhaps Duane Thurston's death and Trevor Sheffield's death were related, and that these deaths might not have been accidental.

The FBI could then pursue that lead, or not, as it saw fit. Angela Forrester would not be mentioned.

After my lunch with Scott, I called Ed, who was now in Los Angeles on a new project, and told him what Scott and I had decided about passing on the information we had acquired in our ramp up to the Texas trial. Ed agreed with our decision and said he would take care of the information transfer, keeping Scott and me and Veronica and Angela Forrester behind the curtain.

My next move in pursuit of my goal to get Scott out from under the legal chaos Duane Thurston had created for him had again to do with the grievance Duane had filed with the Colorado Office of Attorney Regulation Counsel. After a couple of tries, I finally got ahold of Jocelyn Alvarez and told her the person who had filed the grievance against Scott Freeman, Duane Thurston, was dead and I asked her to dismiss the grievance. She requested a death certificate, which my secretary Stephanie was able to provide the next day. In our phone call, Ms. Alvarez told me this wasn't a situation she had ever encountered before, raising the question: does the death of a complaining party terminate a grievance or should the grievance nonetheless be pursued by the Office of Attorney Regulation Counsel? After all, the purpose of the grievance process is to enforce compliance by Colorado lawyers with the Code of Professional Conduct. So, if a violation had in fact occurred, the death of the complaining party wouldn't seem to erase the violation and perhaps discipline of the lawyer involved should continue.

Ms. Alvarez and I had a scholarly debate about this issue in a subsequent phone call and no decision was reached. However, she telephoned me back several days later and told me the Presiding Disciplinary Judge, who is higher up the grievance administration food chain than she is, had reviewed the entire file concerning the grievance against Scott and concluded the grievance should in fact be dismissed, in part because it seemed to be lacking substantial merit in the first place and because the complaining party was no longer around to testify in support of the grievance he had filed, which would make it difficult to prosecute the grievance claim against Scott. A few days later, I received a letter from Ms. Alvarez confirming that the grievance had been dismissed and she had closed her file. I passed this letter on to Scott and he was appropriately relieved. His unblemished record as a fully compliant adherent to the Rules of Professional Conduct remained intact.

"Thanks again, McConnell. You seem to have removed the last big Duane Thurston impediment to my resuming a normal life. Good work."

"Does that mean you've learned your lesson? No more trustee duties?"

"I'm thinking about it. But, you know, my Thurston family assignment isn't quite over yet. As trustee of the Thurston Family Trust, I still need to complete the distributions of PharmOne stock to Phillip and Billie, as the trust agreement requires, further lock Phillip down on a budget with follow up, and make sure there's a long-term support strategy in place for Billie, all of which Maria wanted me to do -- and I promised her I would do -- when I agreed to take over as trustee of the Thurston Family Trust when she died. And, I need to get the Thurston Family Foundation staffed with experienced employees who can carry out its purpose to support cutting edge pharmaceutical research. Folks like that are hard to find these days and in short supply. But Jack, to answer your question, I think I can safely tell you that, after seeing how saying yes to this latest trustee assignment has changed my life, I will be more cautious in the future."

"That's good, Scott, but, you know, I've heard this before, after the Cranston estate controversy, and I'm not sure I believe you."

Since I had planned to be gone all week because of the trial of the Texas lawsuit but had been able to come home early, I decided on Friday I should get back on the softball field with my senior softball teammates. Because of my preparations for Scott's trial, I had missed the last two games. My teammates welcomed me back and told me the team had won those two games. One teammate, in an attempt at humor (I think), said I could take credit for these victories because they wouldn't have been possible if I hadn't been gone and out of the lineup. (Sharing insults was part of the tradition of senior softball.) In this night's game, I redeemed my honor with two doubles and a couple of well-executed defensive plays, and only one botched play where I threw the ball over the first baseman's head and allowed a run to score. In any event, I was invited back to the team's post-game festivities at the Squatting Chicken but I declined. It was time to give Elsie a last visit to the fire plug and head to bed. It had been a long week.

I spent Saturday morning in the office moving piles of paper around in pursuit of a triage strategy. As usual, Stephanie had done a good job keeping clients under control while I was gone and assuring them that I was not, in fact, neglecting their work.

Veronica, just back from Venezuela, came down to Colorado Springs late Saturday afternoon and I was able to get us a last-minute reservation at Le Bistro Saint Tropez, thanks to a cancellation. Because of ever more stringent security protocols, Veronica couldn't tell me all of what was going on in Venezuela, but she was able to tell me enough for me to know that the banking system there was again under attack by S.O.S. She also told me S.O.S. was getting more sophisticated in its ability to hack into government computer networks and position itself to extract concessions in pursuit of curtailing a country's carbon footprint and otherwise saving the planet from global warming. In Venezuela, the people, having suffered from hurricanes, floods, draught and even tornados in recent years, were coming around to being environmental patriots and pressuring the government to take global warming seriously.

Over a second bottle of the white wine from Auxerre we were drinking, I tried to tell Veronica all that had recently happened in Scott Freeman's life. She, like me, was concerned that perhaps we had put Angela Forrester's life in danger with our boots on the ground detective work. But we finally concluded that Angela's knowledge about the pain-medications-diversion-to-the-streets criminal syndicate, which had come from an intoxicated Duane Thurston, would not have been known to the people who took out Thurston and Trevor Sheffield. And, we further concluded that our knowledge of the syndicate, which came from Angela, would not have been known to the bad guys. I did, however, tell Veronica what I had told Scott and Ed – that perhaps my decision to subpoena Trevor Sheffield in the Duane Thurston trial in Texas might raise eyebrows. But, we decided, there were several possible explanations for that subpoena having nothing to do with criminal syndicates and I had not set myself up for a homicide. I told Veronica of Scott's and my decision to have Ed inform the FBI what we had learned from Angela Forrester, but without naming her (or us) as a source, and of our belief that the deaths of Duane Thurston and Trevor Sheffield might not have been accidental. Veronica agreed with our decision and agreed that keeping doors locked was, more than ever, in order.

Chapter 33

With Scott's situation under control, my life returned to its normal level of chaos and Colorado produced for me a near-perfect summer -- no floods, no hailstorms (at least in Colorado Springs), abundant sunshine, blue skies, enough rain to keep the ranchers happy (by their standards), only one wild fire (out near Dinosaur National Monument, where there isn't much to burn in the first place), and stream flows just right for trout habitat.

I took Veronica and Cooper on a couple of enjoyable fishing trips and put in some good solo fishing days, including two overnight trips to high mountain lakes in the San Juan Range where I had the lakes to myself and the cutthroat trout were hungry and active, and liked my Adams 12 flies.

Elsie and I continued to explore local hiking travels on the west side of Colorado Springs, without menacing wildlife encounters. Elsie was proving to be a great hiking companion, in the tradition of Fletcher (only with fewer pee stops).

Cooper had fallen in love with Amy and seemed to have fully recovered from having been dumped by Samantha. He and Amy would regularly pay me a visit at the end of the workday and share time with Elsie and me on my porch.

RJ's estate was wrapped up with no complications and his client files were shredded without repercussions even though the protocols for file retention and client notification were largely ignored. The sale of his house generated a modest inheritance for his children and grandchildren, in keeping with his estate planning aspirations. I regularly used his Orvis 4 weight fly rod and had good memories of RJ every time I did.

In late September, Veronica and I made a trip together back to Vermont to visit her parents. My secretary, Stephanie, assured me she could hold the fort while I was gone and Buttercup welcomed Elsie back for a multi-day sleep over. This trip allowed Veronica's parents, for the first time, to see what their daughter had gotten herself into out in the Wild West. As best I could tell, they concluded I was acceptable. There was, however, something of a tense moment when Veronica's mother suggested we needed separate bedrooms. Veronica handled this nicely by pointing out that separate bedrooms would generate additional laundry, which would consumer precious water resources, better used to irrigate the garden, etc.

Veronica's mother was still running a successful art gallery, attracting customers from New York City and other places. She had started to carry some of Billie Thurston's paintings in her gallery and they were selling well, and had generated positive reviews from snooty East Coast art critics.

Veronica's father, now seventy-five years old but full of life, was in remission from his scary bout with cancer a few years back. He was still teaching physics full time at Middlebury College and was a delightful, twinkle in the eye, storyteller. He was also a fly fisherman and he took me out for a day of fishing on a small nearby stream that not many people knew about. We had a good day catching and releasing 12-inch brook trout, using dry flies big enough to see. Vermont in the fall is a kaleidoscope of colors and they were at their peak on this day. Veronica's father seemed to enjoy the opportunity to spend time with a fellow fly fisher, away from the supervision of his wife. He told me many good stories about Veronica's youth which I had not heard before, and which would give me opportunities, going forward, to bring her back in line when she chose to question my behavior.

Since we were on the East Coast, a place where I'd spent very little time, Veronica and I borrowed her mother's car and drove over to the coast of Maine for a two-day visit. Again, a spectacular venue (although I'm not sure I'd want to be there in January).

When I got back to Colorado, Ed checked in and reported he was working on a couple of interesting new engagements but, as usual, couldn't tell me much about them. He did say, however, that he was looking for further opportunities to use Veronica's skills at espionage in support of his clients' needs for information gathering. He said he had been invited back to Las Vegas for another televised poker tournament and, this time, he ended up with better cards than Shark Face and had come away a winner.

Ed also told me the information he had passed on to the FBI about ExpressRX had led to a bust of the prescription-drugs-sold-on-the-street syndicate. Thus far, six arrests had been made -- two in Colorado, two in Texas, and two in California. Other arrests were likely as the first group to be arrested realized the wisdom of cooperating with the FBI. In all events, the syndicate was, for the moment at least, out of business. But, the national epidemic of drug overdose deaths showed no signs of slowing.

After I was home from the East Coast for a few days, Scott and I got together for another late afternoon meeting at the Antelope Hotel lobby bar. Scott stuck to

Pinot Noir, as did I, and he declined Allie's offer to whip up a to-his-exact ingredients martini.

"Jack, I'm done with that. My heart is doing well and I don't want to mess with it. I have another bet going with Rollie Dumbarton and this time I'm going to win."

"So, Scott, catch me up. What's happening on the Thurston front?"

"All is good. Stella and I have put in place a part time caregiver arrangement for Billie and he is doing great. Phillip has adjusted to, and is still complying with, the budget he and I negotiated. He and Billie have become good friends and are spending quality time together. Phillip was appointed personal representative for Duane Thurston's estate and Duane in fact died intestate, without a will. Duane's assets were enough to cover his debts, although just barely, so his estate was able to pay all creditor claims and his creditors are not a threat to the Thurston Family Trust. Duane's estate actually made a small distribution to Phillip and Billie as Duane's heirs at law. All in all, the Thurston Family Trust is on cruise control and the Thurston Family Foundation is up and running, with a really talented executive staff now in place. Although I'm the CEO, there's not much for me to do. Without a client around to pay him, Manifort, as you know, agreed to dismiss the lawsuit he had filed on behalf of Duane and Billie, and I agreed to dismiss the counterclaim. These dismissals are without prejudice but I'm not worried about the lawsuit coming back to life."

"And what about you?"

"Dr. McMann says I'm almost completely healed from the surgery. I'm walking three miles a day. I have a membership at the Y, like you, and am going there two days a week. Stella has kept me on a heart healthy diet. I haven't had a martini since the surgery, so I am in fact winning my bet with Rollie, although he keeps trying to change the rules. My son Jeff is back teaching and has put together another championship volleyball team for his school. And, I've made some decisions about my life I wanted you to know about."

"OK. I'm sitting down."

"I've learned my lessons about stress. You may not believe this, but I really have been listening to you. And to Rollie. And to Dr. McMann. And to Stella. So, I'm resigning my partnership at Jensen & Kirkpatrick. Starting November 1, I will be 'of counsel' to the firm. This means I won't have first chair client responsibilities anymore. Other lawyers in the firm will do that. I'll be their coach. And, I've been offered a tenured position as a member of the faculty at the University of Colorado law school, and I have accepted that offer. Starting with the winter quarter, I'll be teaching classes on estate planning and taxation."

"Scott, that's wonderful news. Congratulations."

"Yes, but Jack, I do need to tell you about one other thing -- the Stringer trust. For many years, I represented Frank and Melissa Stringer. They were wonderful, kind people and great clients. They're both now dead. I helped them set up a trust as their estate planning vehicle and I agreed to be the trustee of this trust after their death and, well, the beneficiaries of the trust are now in a big fight and, well...."

THE END

ABOUT THE AUTHOR

Jim Flynn grew up in Omaha, Nebraska; attended Dartmouth College on a National Merit Scholarship, majoring in French; and went on to earn a law degree from Stanford Law School. In between the start and finish of law school, Jim served as an officer in the United States Navy, assigned to a branch of the Navy that specializes in electronic espionage, and where he learned Mandarin Chinese. Jim practiced law in Colorado for forty years, both as a transactional lawyer and a litigator. He lives in Colorado Springs, with wife Anne Marie and dogs Jack and Gracie, both Golden retrievers rescued out of Midwest puppy mills. *The Trustee* is a sequel to three earlier Jack McConnell and Veronica Stailey adventures -- *Overdraft*, about a cyber-attack on the U.S. banking system; *Where There's No Will*, about a multi-million dollar will contest in rural Gunnison County, Colorado, which resulted from a missing will; and *Fraudulent Transfers*, about a counterfeit cashier's check fraud and an international money laundering scheme.

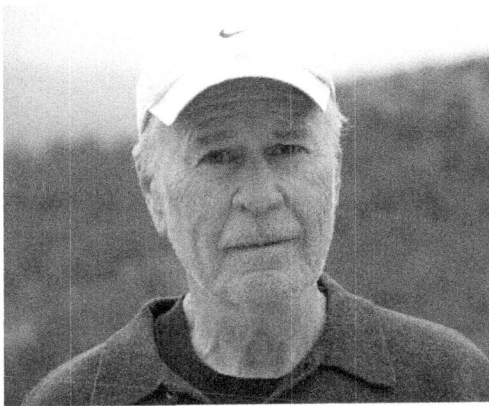

Made in the USA
Las Vegas, NV
01 February 2022